KINGSTON AND THE DRAGON'S COVE

ADAM FREE

CONTENTS

CONTENTS

CHAPTER ONE

The wind blasted quickly, sweeping some bits of dust Kingston's way as he walked down the rocky road, even as the sun pricked at his skin. As Kingston looked up at the sky, he could almost swear that the sun had a frown on its face, as its harshly burned worse by the minute.

"It is pretty hot," Crowly, his pet crow, tucked on his shoulder, remarked with a frown.

"Tell me about it," Kingston said with a groan, just as a group of kids his age passed by him, their laughter ringing in the air and causing some of the adults around to murmur in annoyance under their breaths.

Kingston watched the children his age with a small smile, ignoring the sweat that trailed down his fore-head. They seemed to be having fun, and just looking at them made him think of all the quests he had ever been on.

Kingston tore away his gaze as the children now went into a corner, leaving him standing oddly midway in the town's road. He could feel people watching him, and his cheeks heated in shame, making him drape the hood of the robe he had on further down in an attempt to hide his face.

"Kingston," he heard Crowly's voice shout into his ear, and Kingston jumped in fright before he walked.

"What is it, Crowly?" Kingston's said.

He tucked his hands into the pockets of his robe where he could feel his wand, and he exhaled a bit, his gaze firmly planted on the ground to evade the stares his way. He didn't know where he was even headed at the moment, but he walked on; he didn't feel like going back home, so he took a turn into another street of the town where magical items were sold.

"I could ask you the same thing. You just froze staring at those kids like a creep. Are you ok, Kingston?" Crowly asked with real worry.

A warm smile found its way onto Kingston's face at Crowly's question. He knew that Crowly probably assumed he was sad about seeing kids his age having fun, but what Crowly didn't realize was that Kingston was content at having just Crowly by his side.

"It was nothing, I just recalled some quests of our own while looking at them," Kingston replied, passing by a magic shop that had odd looking runes displayed at its front.

"Hmm," Crowly hummed, following Kingston's gaze which was fixed on the shop.

The place looked rather mystical to Kingston, as he had never seen such relics before, and without thinking any further, Kingston along with Crowly, who was comfortably resting on his shoulder, stepped into the shop, the sound of bells jingling to report the entering of yet another customer.

A quiet gasp escaped both Kingston and Crowly's mouths at the items before them. The shop was filled with odd looking objects and books, with a few customers roaming about, some gathered in a circle and whispering in hushed tones. There was an odd classical look to the shop that made Kingston excited just at the thought of walking past each section of the store.

Kingston walked past the round-bellied man who stood behind the counter at the entrance, reading a book. The man seemed to be a wizard, as Kingston could feel a bit of magical energy around him, though it was pretty weak.

He greeted the man with a nod and went on further to explore some of the shelves in hopes of finding a useful book that could help his magic get stronger.

Kingston almost scoffed out loud as he flipped through a book of magic spells. It claimed to be of advanced level but only contained basic spells. Though anyone could be easily swayed into believing what the book promised, as its contents looked rather hard to understand.

"Did you hear?" He heard an adult lady whisper to her friend just as he placed the book back into its shelf.

Being his usual snoopy self, Kingston stood right beside them in a bid to listen in on whatever their chat was about, while he looked in each book. He knew it was rude to listen to people's gossip, but Kingston simply couldn't help himself. And besides, he planned to walk away if their chat didn't end up being about magic anyway.

"Hear what?"

Kingston picked up another book, his focus now fully on the two ladies beside him.

"Laurie said something about finding a dragon's nest on her visit to the ancient forest some days ago. It seems like the rumors about the last dragon living in that forest are real." The first lady said, and Kingston's eyes expanded at the information.

A dragon's nest?

Did dragons still exist?

"Do you think she's telling the truth?" Crowly whispered into Kingston's ear as he placed the book in his hands onto the shelf, walking along in a bid to hear what the others were talking about.

"I hope so," Kingston whispered back, his eyes shining with hope.

If the rumor about a dragon's nest being in the town's old forest was true, it simply meant a dragon was there.

The ancient forest was known to harbor strange magical creatures and relics. It wasn't like Kingston had never known or thought about going into the forest for a time. It was more like he didn't think it was worth it. But now, hearing of a dragon's existence in the forest was a whole different thing.

A dragon was a powerful magical beast. More powerful than common magical beasts that could be easily defeated by the wave of a wand. It was said that riches and magical knowledge could be gained simply by visiting a dragon's cove.

It was the perfect adventure site for Kingston and Crowly. Kingston only hoped that the rumors were more than just rumors.

The thought of just seeing a dragon face to face made Kingston's insides dance with happiness.

With Crowly now flying right beside him, his black wings sparkling thanks to the sun rays peeking in through the windows of the store, the two friends aimlessly walked around catching more information of the dragon's cove, their earlier joy at exploring the market now replaced by something more.

After listening in to a few more chats that centered on the dragon's existence, Kingston decided it was time to leave the store.

It was hard not to notice how much Kingston was bubbling with excitement. He didn't even mind the sour look the store owner shot at him for leaving the store empty-handed without purchasing anything.

"It's the perfect quest, Crowly. Just think of all the cool stuff we'll find there."

Crowly made a sound of dissent at Kingston's words as he flew right by the young boy's head, mostly covered by a hood. It wasn't that Crowly wasn't excited about going on a quest. It was that they didn't have much info about the time-worn forest.

Even as an expert in all things to do with ruins, Kingston didn't know much about the forest.

"I know but how much do you know about the forest? We don't even know its real name," Crowly reasoned.

Kingston blew out a groan as they started to make their way back "home", where Kingston had been staying for the time being.

The popular wizard of the town, which they were exploring, had invited them over when Kingston and Crowly first arrived at the town to pass time until their next quest.

Crowly stepped into the homely cottage where he found old man Ray, the wizard, mixing up a tonic in the living room. Sweat dripped down the old man's forehead, and he didn't even realize that Kingston and Crowly had been watching him until he turned his head, screaming in surprise.

Kingston and Crowly shared a look before they burst out laughing at the look on the man's face.

After handing Kingston a bowl of cookies to share with Crowly, the wizard listened as Kingston recounted to him what he and Crowly had been up to, making sure to bring up the news of the last dragon.

"Hmm," Old man Ray hummed as he stroked his gray beard. He knew the day would come when Kingston would eventually leave the small town.

That was the life of a wandering wizard, yet the old man adored the child.

The old wizard rose to his feet, leaving Kingston and Crowly confused as he walked into his bedroom. After a few minutes, he returned with a map.

"My family has held onto this map for ages. The old forest you're talking about is home to the dragon's cove. It was said that the dragons lived in that forest for a long time, until they all started to go extinct,"

Kingston and Crowly's eyes went wide open at the wizard's story, making the old wizard chuckle at their faces before he continued.

"If there really is a dragon left in that forest, I can imagine how lonely it must feel. Take care of it. I trust you both to do that."

The two nodded as the old wizard ruffled Kingston's hair and handed the map of the forest to him. They did some research after that as to the kind of magical beasts they would encounter, and the next day, they, along with the old man, went out to get the necessary supplies for their journey.

They got fruits, nuts, healing potions in

case Kingston or Crowly fell ill or got themselves hurt.

When it was time for them to leave, the old wizard hugged Kingston tight.

"Be good, young wizard. Ok?"

Kingston nodded.

The old man then looked to Crowly, who was flying right beside Kingston.

"If anything goes wrong in the forest, make sure to bring him back. I know Kingston can be stubborn, but he listens to you."

Crowly rolled his eyes but nodded anyway. The old man rubbed his head before detaching from his hug with Kingston, and with a wave, turned away to leave.

Kingston smiled cheekily as he watched the old wizard leave. Wizard Ray had been pretty helpful, and he hoped to return with lots of gifts for him. After watching him walk a while down the road, Kingston turned to Crowly as he firmly held onto his backpack.

"Let's go, Crowly, we've got quite the quest ahead of us."

And thus their journey began.

The pair made their way out of the town, with Kingston waving at a few chummy faces and before long, they were out of the tall gates that surrounded the town like a shield.

According to the map old man Ray had

given Kingston, the old forest wasn't so far from the town. It was perhaps the reason few of the townspeople frequently visited the place. Kingston could easily remember how the people at the store he visited the day before, had whispered about the dragon and the forest.

Kingston had to admit, he was filled with both joy and fear.

The pair journeyed through the meadow that stretched far and wide beyond the town muted. Each of them hoped for the quest ahead of them would be full of fun. They had finally arrived at the spot which old man Ray had marked out on the map as the opening to the forest.

"I guess this is it," Kingston mumbled, his

eyes finding those of Crowly's which were stuck to the chilling sight before them.

CHAPTER TWO

The air of the forest hissed with powerful, magic energy, far greater than Kingston and Crowly had ever felt in their lives.

For a moment, it made Kingston stop in his tracks. They had been walking for the past hour, and now they had finally made it to the old forest.

Though it was still very much day, the

opening of the forest was covered in a misty fog that made the trees around the forest look like giant monsters from where Kingston stood. There was also the crackling hue of orange in the sky, a show of how much strong energy was flowing from the forest. It sounded like the rumbling sound of thunder, a sound that had always terrified Kingston for as long as he could remember.

Kingston gulped hard, he looked toward Crowly, who was now shaking slightly.

"We can't back down now, Crowly," Kingston told him, even if really, he was talking to himself.

They had come this far; they couldn't just run back because they were scared.

"I-I didn't say I was scared," Crowly shivered.

The shining sun didn't provide enough warmth to help against the cold that covered the forest, thus the reason Crowly was shivering and the reason Kingston hugged his magic robe tighter to his body.

Kingston got out his magic wand that had been safely put in his pocket. He needed to clear the fog away because it acted as some kind of blocker to the sun. It would be harsh if they had to put up with the cold for much longer. Plus, they could become the victims of attack from magical beasts. The exotic magical beasts were one of the reasons the forest's magical energy was so strong.

"Fog, fog, go aloft," Kingston waved his wand into the air, hoping that his magic would be enough to clear away the strong fog.

A mighty rush of wind from the tip of his wand caused him and Crowly to inch back a bit as it grew larger, until it swept away the fog oozing out of every corner of the forest, and in a matter of seconds, the two friends were welcomed to the true sight of the forest.

Now that the fog was gone, they could clearly see the trees surrounding them like a cage, along with some cute furry magical beasts roaming the grounds and trees.

Kingston and Crowly shared a look, big smiles on their faces.

With the fog gone, the forest looked more welcoming and pretty, adorned with the vibrant color of green.

"Let's go," Kingston whispered, and they walked on the ground filled with shining pebbles.

Occasionally as they walked, Kingston would stop to pick up things he found gripping.

Like the multi-colored fur he found peeking out from a hole in a tree. Kingston assumed the fur was owned by one of the odd birds with the same multi-colored fur flying high over the forest.

Everything seemed to be going great, but the more ground they went over, the greater the magic energy became.

"Is it just me or does the forest look way wider than how it did on the map Mr. Ray gave to us?" Crowly set forth his concern after a while.

The map the old wizard handed to them made the forest look way smaller than it really was.

Crowly suspected that the amount of magical energy in the forest was doing something to the place. Perhaps making the place wider, making it hard for them to reach the dragon. That, or they were super lost.

Crowly heard the sound of paper crumpling and when he turned his slender crow's neck. He found Kingston going through the map with a frown on his face.

"You're right, Crowly, but we're way past the entry way now," Kingston tucked back the paper into his pockets. "We just have to-"

"Kingston, look out!" Crowly cut off Kingston's words with a yell as a huge monster flew right above Kingston's head, taking him and Crowly by surprise.

The two friends, with their hearts pounding, turned in fright to find the monster had flown to one of the trees. It was a Griffin.

A Griffin, just like a dragon, was a scant magical beast that could only be found in highly magical forests such as this.

An odd beast with the body of a lion and the head, wings, and talons of an bird.

Kingston knew he couldn't engage in a fight with such a beast whose bird-like eyes looked right back at him and Crowly.

"They're everywhere," Crowly said as he craned his neck to find more Griffins at corners of the forest watching them.

Kingston knew that the Griffin had likely been alarmed by the sound their feet made against the ground. They were all highly alert, watching Kingston's every move. If Kingston were to make any wrong move, they'd attack him all at once.

"We can't fight them," Crowly said, inching closer to Kingston who held his wand tightly against his chest.

Kingston whispered back with a slight eye roll. "I know,"

Though if Kingston really wanted, he might win in a fight, but they didn't have the luxury of time to waste. The light the sun had provided them was now getting dim by every passing hour.

"I'll just have to distract them instead,"

And then with a wave of his wand, Kingston summoned falling stones.

"Stone, stones. Let it rain stones."

The sound and sight of plentiful stones of all sizes shocked the Griffins, and while trying to evade them, Kingston and Crowly used the moment to run out from that part of the forest, passing through another trail from what Old man Ray had circled out for them.

If they went further off the trail, there was the risk of them getting lost. Well, more lost.

Kingston panted, a sigh escaping his lips. It wasn't like he had a choice. It was either traveling off course or fighting those Griffins and drawing more hazards to themselves.

"Kingston,"

29

Kingston groaned, sweat trailing down his forehead. He was still trying to comport himself after all the running. He could not even get a proper word out.

"Kingston," Came Crowly's voice, more urgent this time and Kingston's head shot up in worry only for his eyes to widen at the sight before him.

The air was covered with golden dust trailing after tiny colorful beasts roaming about.

Fairies? Pixie dust?

He didn't know what to make of the little glowing beats buzzing around them like fire-flies. They made the entire spring glow with charm. Yet, Kingston could feel the trail of powerful magic that made his insides shiver.

Crowly's eyes gave Kingston's a look before they both whispered at the same time.

"The dragon,"

There was a pond of water by shimmering stones and the air was covered with what Kingston assumed to be pixie dust from the little fairies roaming about.

One even came so close to him, he felt like a giant in contrast to the little beast whose wings reminded him of glass. It buzzed in his ears likely trying to tell him something. But he, sadly, didn't speak fairy. Learning to speak the lingo of other beats was now part of Kingston's bucket list though.

"Should we go check for some hints?" Crowly asked, watching with awe as the colorful fairies surrounded him and tugged at his wings. They seemed enchanted by how black and shiny his wings were.

They didn't seem unsafe. And it seemed like they were inviting the pair to spend some time with them.

Kingston thought for a while. The tip of his wand tapping his chin. Compared to when they were faced with Griffins, fairies had less magical energy around them. Meaning they were likely harmless. But if they were all to attack together, they might overpower him.

Though, Kingston didn't think the fairies thought of that.

Also, he felt the presence of a powerful beast. Even the Griffin's energy didn't compare to what Kingston was feeling from something close by.

The dragon had been here.

The dragon was real.

"There's no need for hints," Kingston stated, placing his wand back into his robe and slipping off the backpack he had on his back.

"So what now? Should we leave and come back in the morning?" Crowly asked.

"Nope," Kingston replied, the 'p' popping. "It's getting dark. Let's just stay here until tomorrow. What do you say buddy?"

After dropping his backpack by a tree trunk, Kingston made his way to the pond.

Darkness was now setting in and the sun had now been replaced by the moon. It looked beautiful from the pond where Kingston could see it more plainly.

The moon looked like it winked at him and Kingston got a shiver from the sight. Maybe the magic energy was playing tricks on his mind.

"..... Ok I don't mind." Crowly said, with a tad bit of distress.

He found Kingston sitting by the pond

and flew to where he was before landing on the sandy spot beside the boy.

They had known each other for years but there were times Crowly couldn't just guess what Kingston was thinking. Most times Crowly was bothered about Kingston feeling alone and it made Crowly wish that he wasn't just a bird.

"Everything alright, kiddo?"

Kingston turned with a grin just as his belly rumbled and he blushed.

"Well, I am a bit hungry."

Crowly rolled his eyes before he left Kingston's side to get the backpack which had their food.

He placed it beside Kingston who muttered a thank you before unzipping the backpack and biting into an apple. His eyes returned to the beautiful pond. Some fairies were now hovering slightly above the pond making it sparkle even more.

"I bet the dragon comes here to take baths,"

Crowly snorted at Kingston's statement. "Take baths? I don't think dragons do that Kingston. Maybe he comes here to spend time with the fairies though. They are pretty cool."

Kingston pouted. He liked the idea of a mighty dragon feeling the water on its scales but Kingston knew Crowly was right. And besides, the pond was too small for even a baby dragon.

"Whatever," Kingston mumbled as he went to munch on his dinner of apples and Crowly smiled fondly at him.

Ever since Kingston had learned that his parents were wizards who always went on quests, Crowly noticed that Kingston wanted to do the same.

The town's people had tried their best to take care of Kingston but he never felt like he belonged back in the small town, especially on days when he heard stories about feats his parents had done. And so, that was how Kingston's story really began.

His quest to be a great, great wizard.

And at each step of the way, Crowly had been there. He was a gift handed to Kingston at his four-year-old birthday and they had been best friends ever since. Crowly chuckled at the memories that flooded his head as he sat beside Kingston who started to hum a song.

The night was cool. The trees swayed and the young wizard and his pet enjoyed every bit of it, ignorant of what the future had in store for them.

CHAPTER THREE

It was the soft gust of wind on Kingston's hair that woke him up, along with
Crowly who kept pecking him with his
beak. Kingston stirred in anger but refused to open his eyes. He knew they had
to continue their journey but he felt so
relaxed lying on the soft sand.

If he had the chance, he wouldn't even
mind simply lying down the entire day.

"Come on, Kingston, you have got to wake up," Crowly nagged at him, and Kingston groaned before he finally opened his eyes to find Crowly looking right into his face.

"I'm up Crowly, Gosh. I've told you to stop using your beak on me; it hurts," Kingston complained before his eyes roamed around the place.

Now that it was daytime, Kingston could not see any of the fairies, but it felt as though they were being watched, and Kingston concluded that the fairies were probably hiding in the trees.

"Sorry Kingston, but it's the only way I can always get you to wake up."

Crowly had tried other methods in the past and none of them ever seemed to work except whenever he pecked on Kingston. It seemed to annoy him a lot.

Kingston shook his head with an eye roll as he got up to his feet. The night before was a special night to Kingston, and as he looked at the pond which reflected the sun's light and his features of curly black hair and brown eyes, Kingston hoped to never forget such a day..

After drinking some water from the pond, Kingston grabbed his backpack from the floor just as Crowly came down on his shoulder. The pet crow felt bad for having to wake Kingston up, but it had been hours since the sun came up and they had a lot of ground to cover if they were to find the Dragon's cove.

"Ready to leave?" Crowly asked Kingston who still seemed a bit sleepy, and Kingston nodded his head in reply.

Right before stepping onto another trail leading further into the forest, Kingston stuck his head into one of the openings in the trees to find the fairies who had showed them kindness. Just like he had thought, they were indeed hidden in the trees, roaming around in it like it was some kind of mini town to them.

"Thanks guys," Kingston loudly said with a grin before retracting his head in order to continue his quest.

The trees swayed as the buzzing sound the fairies usually made grew stronger until Kingston could clearly hear fourteen words slowly and carefully spoken together in unison.

"Good luck on your quest kids; we hope to see you some other time."

Kingston's face burned with an odd feeling as he laughed along with Crowly who couldn't believe his ears. As they exited the pond areas, Kingston couldn't stop the amazing feeling of having fairies speak to him, especially using human words.

"I definitely didn't expect them to say anything. I didn't even think they could understand us," Crowly remarked, gazing back at the pond right before it went away from his view.

"Me neither. I bet they tried all night long just to make it sound special for us," Kingston smiled warmly.

The forest wasn't all bad, though sometimes he could feel the hair on his body rise due to the feeling of being watched by evil monsters. But there were also good magical monsters too.

Kingston hoped that they would not have to be faced with an evil magical beast or wizard as they went along in their quest. All he wanted was to have fun.

And so the pair moved in a slow, quiet, tone, taking stops to drink water and eat nuts from Kingston's backpack.Oddly, there was even more food than they started their quest with. This almost made Kingston cry knowing it was the fairies' handiwork. Crowly had to keep him from running back to go thank them as the young wizard's heart had been filled with warmth at the fairies' act of kindness.

Their quest was going rather peaceful as Kingston hoped until they reached a part of the forest that was covered with the same intense fog that had blocked off the forest's entrance when they first arrived.

Kingston halted in his tracks as a deep frown found its way to his face. It wasn't the fog that bothered him. That, he could easily brush off with his wand.

It was the thought of a magical beast watching them from beyond the fog that worried the young wizard. Its shining orange eyes could be clearly seen and Kingston inched back as his hands started to feel his pockets for his wand.

"There's something there," Crowly said into Kingston's ear. But as Crowly said it, it felt like the magical beast could hear him.

Every breath they took, every step they made, and every word that slipped out of their mouths.

It could hear everything.

Kingston knew that if they tried to evade

this path like they had done the day before with the Griffins, they'd be knocked
off course.

"We have to-"

Kingston's eyes widened in shock as the
flying beast came from the fog charging
towards him in full force, and he dashed
behind a tree just as Crowly flew off his
shoulders.

"Crowly, run," Kingston yelled as the
beast, which was now seen to be a gargoyle, knocked itself into one of the
trees, missing Kingston simply by chance.

'Run?' Crowly thought to himself in annoyance. There was no way he was going

to leave Kingston behind. And so he began picking and throwing stones at the
gargoyle whose roar made the pair trem-
ble in their boots.

The magical energy that surrounded the
beast was far more than what Kingston
had felt so far. It was like the deeper
they went into the forest, the worse
magical beasts they came across.

"I told you to run," Kingston moaned,
watching Crowly throw stones at the
Gargoyle which seemed to be getting
madder by the second.

The beast once again charged towards
Kingston, showing its dog-like body at
Kingston who shuddered at the sight. It
was simply an animal yet it felt so evil.

Kingston could even see the saliva dripping from its teeth.

His hands shook in fright.

A magical genius he was, but he wasn't the best at fighting a beast he had never come across before.

And so instead of using his powers, he ducked out of the Gargoyle's way as his mind thought on the perfect spell he could use to defeat the monster.

He couldn't keep ducking forever. Kingston knew that the monster knew that and so it didn't mind playing the game of tag with Kingston.

"Kingston," Crowly yelled as he kept picking up more stones to throw at the

Gargoyle, but his mouth fell open when he saw the ball of fire charging out of its mouth toward Kingston. It all happened in slow motion in Crowly's eyes and it was one of the moments he wished he was a human so he could push Kingston out of the way.

All he could do right at the moment was hope, hope with tears brimming in his eyes that nothing would happen to Kingston.

"Stop, block, pop up," Kingston managed to yell quickly even while in shock, and the Gargoyle's ball of fire was blocked off by the shield that went around Kingston. Yet the force of the fireball knocked Kingston down, putting him on his back.

This was bad. Very bad.

Kingston knew he had to think fast and attack instead of defend, but the monster was far too fast and Kingston had to get on his feet before the monster could shoot another fire ball.

"Use a glamor spell Kingston. Something, anything," Crowly yelled before he started to use his beak to attack the monster which kept swatting him away. Crowly knew he had to act. He would do anything to protect Kingston.

Meanwhile, Crowly's words kept bouncing about in Kingston's mind.

Glamor?

A glamor of what?

And besides, making glamors was a pretty hard spell to do. Kingston didn't even think he could remember the right words to speak because they weren't normal words like he used all the time.

And then like a bucket of ice dropped on him, an idea struck Kingston.

He could make thousands of copies of himself and Crowly.

If all the copies attacked the monster at once, they would distract him.

And so right as Kingston evaded yet another blast of fire balls rapidly shot at him, he waved his wand in the air screaming the strange magic words in the air, not caring if even the dragon could hear him.

"Tow, top, migica, alifa aLie"

Just as he said the odd words, copies of himself and Crowly started to appear out of nowhere until the Gargoyle was surrounded by thousands of Kingstons and Crowlys.

The monster growled in fluster and anger as it now started to randomly shoot fireballs at each copy only to have them vanish and multiply.

While the beast struggled to make sense of what was happening, the real Crowly flew toward Kingston.

Kingston placed a finger in front of his lip to stop Crowly from saying anything, and while the Gargoyle battled with their copies, the pair quietly walked away.

They didn't speak a word until they were sure they were out of the Gargoyle's reach.

"That was a close one," Kingston said, leaning on a tree, but he quickly backed away at the thought of yet another creature lurking behind it.

"Tell me about it," Crowly said back, shaking his head that had ashes on it. If Crowly had not been careful, he would have been cooked meat by now.

The thought alone made the crow feel chills. They had escaped the Gargoyle by a hair's length.

"So what now?" Crowly asked using his

wings to help dust off ashes from Kingston too. They both reeked of smoke.

Crowly didn't even know Kingston could
make that many copies. When he said a
glamor, he thought the boy would make
just a few copies. But it was way better
than he ever could have hoped for.

The child was really a genius, and Crowly
was proud of him.

"Well, we'll keep up our quest. Though-"
Kingston got out the map from his pocket
which had now been blackened by smoke.
Kingston could have simply done a reverse spell on the paper if he had seen it
quicker, but it was already too late.

Reverse spells could only be done a few

55

minutes after the damage had been done.

"The map is ruined," Kingston gasped and lifted up his eyes to take in the truth before them.

Kingston's brow raised up as he saw strange forms in the distance. Some looked just like the Gargoyle they had just faced. Scary.

Without thinking, Kingston started to walk toward the ruins in a bid to assess them, and Crowly turned his head to what Kingston was looking at, his little crow eyes widening.

"Whoa," Crowly gasped.

"It's like the more we walk, the crazier the things we see," Kingston remarked.

It seemed to him like some old city that had been long abandoned.

There was a pyramid-like shape at the center, right by trees with vines shooting out from each corner. It was the only place that looked somewhat like it could be explored.

Kingston slowly walked around the scrap of stones that were by the pyramid, jumping over the litter until the shimmering blue-green colors of shed dragon scales and large footprints on the ground made Kingston and Crowly trade a knowing look.

The dragon had been there and they were getting closer to it.

CHAPTER FOUR

"It's around here somewhere, I can feel it in my bones," Kingston rubbed his chin as he watched Crowly fly around, surveying the area for more clues.

Though he could not feel the dragon's magical energy anymore, Kingston didn't think much of it. Magical beasts were known to hide their magical power whenever they felt like it.

Kingston sighed. His back still hurt from his fall before, and so he rested on one of the dragon scales hoping nothing bad would happen. The last thing he wanted was to get into another heated battle with a magical beast. They could be pretty scary.

"Well, the footprints seem to have vanished, so unless you cast some spell to track them, we're at a dead end," Crowly said with a shrug.

Kingston groaned at Crowly's words. Kingston was tired. Casting a powerful magic spell, such as the illusion spell, drained him of most of his magical energy for the time being. And he needed to rest up to get it back. He slipped down to the ground, shrugging off his backpack which had been on him the entire time.

Hopefully, the nuts which the fairies had gifted to them were not crushed. He would be sad if that were the case. He didn't think their act of kindness could melt his heart the way it did, and Kingston was simply afraid at the thought of anything happening to their gifts.

Kingston drew in a sharp breath as he unzipped the bag just as Crowly, now finished with his survey, flew back to Kingston's side.

A relieved sigh escaped his lips as the berries, apples, and other gifts from the fairies remained whole. Kingston didn't even realize that a tear-drop had dripped down his eyes until he felt Crowly's feather wipe the tear away.

"It's ok, Kingston. Everything ended up fine and will continue to be fine," Crowly assured Kingston as he proceeded to plop a berry into Kingston's wide-opened mouth.

After chewing on the berry, Kingston spoke in a low, tone. "I know, Crowly, I guess I was just really happy about seeing everything safe. I was scared. Those fairies were so kind to us, losing their gifts and the things we picked up would've been like missing a part of this journey."

Crowly nodded in understanding but didn't say anything as Kingston continued to eat his berries.

It was almost noon by the time Kingston felt refreshed and ready to continue his quest with Crowly; though he had dozed off. Kingston thought back to the Gargoyle and hoped that the monster was worn out from having to constantly fight fake illusions.

As Kingston rose to his feet, Crowly was startled out of his sleep and Kingston chuckled at the alarmed look on his face as his head turned back and forth as though he was expecting to find that they were under attack.

His eyes finally found those of Kingston's and Crowly sighed.

"I can't believe I dozed off. I was supposed to be watching you," Crowly muttered, using his wings to rub his sleepy eyes.

Kingston snorted in reply, slinging his backpack over his shoulder.

"You're not my watcher, Crowly. You needed that sleep."

Kingston walked forward to pick up some of the scrap from the ruins and waved his wand in the air after to further track where the footprints which had vanished went to.

"Foot prints, Footprints, lead me to the end of your trail,"

More footprints appeared on the muddy

ground leading past the pyramid structure into some other part of the forest.

Kingston turned his neck to Crowly with
a grin.

"Let's go find that dragon, Crowly."

Crowly flew right behind Kingston as they
both followed the new set of trails pushing past overgrown weeds and litter along
their way until they made it to the glade
where the trail ended.

It was like a wonderful garden.

The spot where Kingston and Crowly had
found the fairies couldn't compare to the
amazing beauty before them.

It felt as though they were standing in a
museum with artifacts from long ago on

full display.

There was a waterfall, the sound of gushing water surrounding the area and filling the pair with excitement. The trees here were of kinds Kingston had only ever heard about in books.

Flowers and plants of different kinds adorned the place. Ranging from daisies to roses, tulips and many more Kingston couldn't even spot.

And at the center of all the beauty, was a large nest with a golden egg that looked like it had been cracked open for quite some time.

But even with all the beauty around him, Kingston felt that something was very wrong.

He didn't think of it before but now that they were finally at the dragon's cove, the question burned in his mind.

Why couldn't he feel the dragon's magical energy any longer?

The day before he could strongly feel it. It was such a powerful feeling and almost impossible to ignore. But ever since he opened his eyes that morning, he couldn't feel it any longer.

And now, only faint traces remained.

Why wasn't the dragon at it's nest?

Where was the dragon they had been searching so desperately for?

"Something's wrong isn't it?" Crowly said with a sigh as he noticed the look on Kingston's face.

Couldn't they at least just catch a break?

"Or perhaps the dragon went for a swim or-"

"No," Kingston cut Crowly's sentence short as he ran his hand through his curly hair.

"If the dragon were still in this forest I would have felt its energy. I felt it at the pond. I felt it even at the entrance of the forest. But now, it's completely gone."

Crowly felt the urge to smack himself on the face. Where could the dragon have possibly gone?

"Let's split up and check for clues. I bet even if the dragon flew away, it shouldn't have gone far. Besides," Kingston looked over at the cracked egg. "Its still pretty much a baby,"

Crowly nodded and flew off to look around, while Kingston did the same with the help of his magic. It helped to track and uncover anything that was supposed to seem hidden in plain sight.

Crowly looked around the dragon's nest, his eyes widening when all the riches he had heard could be found at a dragon's nest were nowhere to be found.

There was no gold, no fancy dragon nails, no magical book of spells.

It was all gone.

Almost like someone had...

"Kingston, over here," Crowly cried out. Kingston rushed over to the other side where Crowly had been checking, and when his eyes made contact with those of Crowly's, he followed Crowly's gaze back to what he had been looking at.

There were footprints.

But not just any kind of footprints. The footprint they had followed the first time was larger than that of a human's and oddly shaped too, but right now, what Kingston was looking at seemed to be the footprint of any normal human. Of an adult perhaps, with how large it looked.

The person seemed to have tried to hide it but did a pretty bad job. Kingston could see small traces of it before it totally vanished.

Kingston's hands shook. He couldn't tell or understand what he was feeling at the moment.

Was it anger at coming this far only to find the cove abandoned? Or rage at the fact that a human just like him had been here and most probably stole all the riches that would normally be at a dragon's nest.

Did the strange person also have a hand in the dragon's fading?

His mind reeled on.

Perhaps it was that lady at the store talking about her friend Laurie or someone from the town, but the towns-people viewed the old forest as a sacred place.

No one would think of stealing or kidnapping a dragon.

"So what now, Kingston? Whoever left this trail did so quite recently. Look at the trail, it's still pretty fresh."

Kingston sighed, "But we would've known if there was another human in here. We would've crossed paths one way or the other. Unless..." Kingston's brows furrowed.

Unless, if there was another entrance into the forest no one else knew about.

If the forest had a beginning, it also had to have an end.

And then, Kingston drew the verdict of the matter. It was not the townspeople. They totally did not have a hand in the dragon's vanishing. It was someone else. Someone with vast info about the forest and about the dragon.

Anyone who could successfully kidnap a dragon was an evil wizard in Kingston's book, and he was going to make sure such a person was brought to justice.

"Let's follow the trail. I'm pretty sure it'll lead us to the dragon."

Crowly seemed a bit unsure of Kingston's words. The quest had changed now, and

Crowly thought it better to turn around and go back home. But he knew there was no way Kingston would listen to advice like that. Kingston had a strong sense of justice, and would do everything to get the dragon back safely to its home.

It was one of the many things Crowly loved about Kingston. Because if it were up to Crowly, he'd fly back home without a second thought.

"Alright then," Crowly said with a sad sigh.

Kingston raised a brow at him as he got out his wand to track the trails which had been hidden.

"I thought you'd try to talk me into going

back," Kingston smiled, his anger at the scene fading at Crowly's willingness to continue the journey.

Crowly rolled his eyes as he perched on the young wizard's shoulder.

"It's not like I have much of a choice. Let's hope that when we find the dragon, it doesn't try to turn us into steak."

Kingston laughed heartily at Crowly's joke before waving his wand in the air.

"Footprints, footprints, show yourself."

The rest of the human's footprints along with the strange ones of the dragons popped up, leading out of the cove right through the waterfall. It was strange that the trail led them toward the waterfall, and Kingston turned his head a bit to give Crowly an hesitant look.

Crowly shrugged his shoulders, and with a sigh, the young wizard went ahead to follow the trail, wondering what he would find beyond the waterfall.

CHAPTER FIVE

A vexed groan left Kingston's mouth as he walked through the waterfall that drenched his and Crowly's bodies with water. Though drying off the water with magic wasn't a hassle for him, he still hated the cold feeling that passed through his entire body and the fact that his robes were dripping wet at the moment.

Kingston wiped the water off his face

that blocked his view of what was before them as Crowly shook his feathers to dry off the water on him.

As soon as the drops of water were off Kingston's eyes, he let out a surprised remark.

"Whoa, Crowly. You have to see this."

At Kingston's words, Crowly halted his actions, turning his attention to what Kingston was looking at, and his beak opened a bit.

Crowly could see the faint outline of buildings. It reminded him of something.

Crowly then gasped. Was that a school in the hills they were looking at? Or was it simply an illusion, Crowly wondered as

Kingston started to move forward, not minding the fact that he was still very much drenched with water.

Even though they stood quite a distance from the school hidden in the hills, Kingston could faintly see people walking and a few flying on their brooms. The sight filled Kingston with a thrill of joy.

When he walked through the waterfall, a school structure was the last thing he expected they would see. He thought the trail would perhaps lead them to a secret cave or right to the culprit who had kidnapped the dragon.

"Wait a minute, Kingston. Where do you think you're going?" Crowly asked, flying off Kingston's shoulder to block him from walking forward.

Kingston blinked at Crowly's question, turning his neck a bit to find that he had walked a distance from the waterfall toward the school on the hills.

Kingston's cheeks warmed. He hadn't even thought things through.

"Don't tell me you just plan to waltz into the school like we didn't just find out about its existence a few seconds ago. There's a reason it's hidden out here, Kingston."

"I know," Kingston sighed, now realizing how sticky and heavy his clothes and backpack felt. He quickly cast a spell with his wand to help dry out all the water on him and once he was done, he returned his attention to Crowly who had his beak pursed in a manner that seemed both funny and serious to Kingston.

"We have to come up with a plan," Crowly continued, and Kingston nodded as his eyes found the trail of the dragon and culprit continuing right down until it disappeared right into the hills.

"Yes, and that plan is to infiltrate the school." Kingston replied.

Crowly rolled his eyes. "So what are you gonna say when the school workers question you at the gate? Let me guess, 'Oh hi guys my name is Kingston and I happen to be a super smart wizard who wants to

save a dragon that was stolen by someone from this school.'"

Kingston face-palmed. "You know there's
no way I can say that. And I don't sound
like that either, Crowly." He said under
his breath.

"Good, we seem to be on the same page."
Crowly nodded his head and then moved
closer to Kingston. "So what then do you
plan on telling them, and how are you going to hide the strong magical energy surrounding you?"

A frown graced Kingston's face as he
thought long and hard. The sun was starting to set as it slowly hid behind the
clouds, and Kingston knew he had to think

fast. Magical energy could only be perceived by powerful wizards. To them, it looked like a cloud of mist surrounding a person, and Kingston reckoned that the school hidden in the hills was probably packed with powerful wizards like him who could spot him out at a single look.

That was his only problem at the moment. Sneaking into the school would be easy. He could simply pose as a new student and hide all his expert magical skill by acting dull and dumb. But if they were going to believe him, he needed to hide the strong magical energy around him.

But, how could he hide it?

"Think, Kingston. Think." The young wizard whispered to himself. He had never had to hide his powers before, as no event had ever called for it. So it was a bit hard for him to come up with an idea.

Crowly opened his mouth to suggest they abort their quest of sneaking into the school for the day. But Kingston beat him to talking as he raised a finger in the air.

"I've got it," Kingston exclaimed, and Crowly sighed, imagining a lighted bulb hovering over Kingston's head.

"I haven't tried this before, but I could cast an glamor spell on myself to appear as a normal wizard."

Crowly narrowed his eyes, tilting his head to the side as he looked into Kingston's excited brown eyes.

Was that even possible? Crowly thought to himself.

"Right," Crowly drawled out and then quickly added. "But I won't be able to tell if the spell works or not, Kingston, since I'm not a wizard, so it's quite a risky plan."

Kingston shrugged. He didn't have any other choice, and he was running out of time. And so before Crowly could say anything else, Kingston waved his wooden-woven wand in the air. He didn't even know the right words to chant, so he used the same words he had used when he had faced off with the gargoyle, hoping it'll work.

A bright light flashed from his wand, and then, that was it. Kingston expected something grand to happen, but felt wholly nothing. He gulped as his eyes found those of Crowly's before the pet crow began to fly forward.

"That spell had better worked, Kingston. Or else it's over." Crowly commented and with a sigh. Kingston picked up his pace to match with Crowly who flew ahead toward the school on the hill.

The walk out of the old forest and down the path leading to the hill was silent as Kingston navigated through the vast land.

The sight was truly the world at its best, and Kingston had to remind himself of the quest at hand as the grass tickled his feet, tempting him to lie and spread out his arms and legs while covered in the grass.

As they got closer to the school, Kingston could now clearly make out some buildings. From afar, the school looked tiny, but now some feet from its entrance, Kingston and Crowly felt as though the large golden gates would open up its mouth and swallow them whole.

Kingston also realized that even with the spell he had cast on himself, he could still very much feel a large amount of magical energy oozing off from the school's gates.

It made Kingston a bit bothered if the spell worked at all.

He traded a nervous glance with Crowly,

who then flew over, perching on his shoulder.

"Everything alright? We could always turn back." Crowly asked, looking at how rigid Kingston seemed.

Kingston didn't want to worry Crowly, and so he shook his head, muttering a "I'm fine," before tightening his grip on the strap of his backpack as he started to move forward to the gate with the name 'Wizard Academy' boldly shimmering even with the setting sun.

As soon as Kingston reached the gates and stretched out his hand to knock, a beeping sound came from the other side, scaring the young wizard. He took a step back just as the gates came open.

At first, Kingston could not see anything until he heard a tiny voice coming from the ground.

"I'm over here."

With his brows scrunched, he looked down to find a person way shorter than him wearing a patrol uniform. Two more emerged from the gates, each holding a wand which seemed far more fancy than Kingston's.

"State your business, kid, or we blast you," The first patrolman stated with a mean look on his face. Though Kingston thought he was a bit cute.

"Uh, my name is Kingston. I'm here to enroll to uh, better my magical skills," Kingston stuttered, gulping afterward as he continued to stare into the patrolman's stern blue eyes.

The patrolman narrowed his eyes with concern before turning to look at the other two guards with him, and after whispering among themselves, they all went back through the gate.

"I don't think they believed me," Kingston whispered to Crowly right before the gates came fully open, revealing the entire school to Kingston, whose eyes glinted at the sight.

Though the buildings weren't as many as he had assumed they were, they still managed to look just as amazing. They were made of fine red-colored bricks with a dragon-shaped fountain at the center which had water that seemed like fire coming out of the dragon's mouth.

There were also the voices of children coming from blocks away and some elderly wizards flying on their brooms.

The school was everything Kingston could ever imagine and more.

"This way, Kid." One of the patrolmen nudged his leg. With a small nod and a trade of glances with Crowly, Kingston started to move forward.

They walked past some buildings, taking turns left and right until the patrolman stopped right in front of a building that had the name 'office' boldly flashing in colors of blue. Kingston reckoned the flashing effect the letters made was as a result of magic.

A large grin grew on Kingston's face as the guard turned to tell him something but they were stopped by the sound of the wooden grand doors of the building opening, showing a rather tall lady wearing a blue robe with a pointy black hat on her head. He also saw she was holding a magic flying broomstick in her hands. And as her brown eyes made contact with those of Kingston's, her brow furrowed.

Kingston's heart raced a little at the thought of the lady being able to sense his magical energy.

"And who might you be?"

"About that, Ms. Hats," The patrolman, without sparing another glance at Kingston, ran up the four steps of the stairs and started to whisper into the lady's ears.

"It'll be alright, Kingston," Crowly said to him right as the patrolman returned from speaking to the lady and walked past Kingston without another word.

"Uh-" Kingston turned and began to call out to the patrolman but was interrupted by the lady who clapped her hands to catch his regard.

"Go back home, kid. You can come back with your parents tomorrow, but for now, follow me in to grab an enrollment form for your parents to fill out," The lady said as she pointed with her hands for Kingston to come meet her.

Kingston gulped.

He definitely could not go back. Not after they had come this far. And who was this lady, anyway? She could not just decide to kick him out.

Kingston concluded that he'd try everything he could to convince her to let him in the school as he started up the stairs. Standing in front of her, he now realized how tall she really was. She gave Kingston a once-over before opening the wooden doors to the building and stepping in.

Kingston tailed behind her still with Crowly on his shoulder. No one seemed to have noticed the pet crow yet, and if they did, they likely didn't mind.

"Ms. Hats, if you don't mind, I'd love it if I could enroll today. You see-"

"I totally can not enroll you without the approval of a parent, Kid," Ms. Hats replied, turning to look at Kingston as they walked down the empty hallways before leading to an office that had the nameplate, 'Principal' on it.

"But-"

"But, it's the rule, Kid," Mrs. Hats said with a sigh, unlocking the door to her office and ushering Kingston in.

"My name is Kingston." Kingston cor-
rected her with a grumble.

With a frown on his face, Kingston bit
down on his bottom lip as he watched
Mrs. Hats briskly walking towards her
large desk. Her office looked quite a bit
more modern than what Kingston was
used to seeing. There also wasn't anything quite magical about it.

Kingston had to think of a way to let Mrs.
Hats enroll him immediately. He definitely
couldn't return to the forest as the sun
had already set. It was far too late for
him now.

So, Kingston said the only thing he could
possibly think of at the moment.

"I'm an orphan, and I really have nowhere else to go if you send me back,"

Mrs. Hats sharply turned from the documents she was looking through to Kingston, whose eyes were brimming with tears.

She hated to see children cry. It was totally Mrs. Hat's weak point, and learning that the kid was an orphan made her strong choice of him enrolling the next day waver.

She sighed, looking Kingston over. He sure did look scrawny with a pet crow on his shoulder. And from his clothes, she could tell that he hadn't taken a bath for days.

Without asking Kingston any further questions, Mrs. Hats, with the help of her delivery bird pet, sent a message to the wizard in charge of the boys' dorm to come attend to Kingston.

"How old are you, Kingston?" She asked, once she had sent off her pigeon.

Kingston's cheeks flushed in discomfort. He didn't really like telling his age, but at the moment, he thought it was important he told Mrs. Hats.

"Twelve, Mrs. Hats."

With a small smile, Mrs. Hats walked over to where Kingston stood, clasping her hands behind her back and leaning over to Kingston.

"Well then, welcome to the Wizard Academy, Kingston."

CHAPTER SIX

After Mrs. Hats welcomed him into the school, Kingston was handed over to the wizard in charge of the boys' dorm, Mr. Patrick, who came minutes after, leading him out of Mrs. Hats' office.

He then put Kingston through the placement tests of the school. According to Mr. Patrick, Kingston enrolled at the right time as they were not too deep into the school's curriculum.

Kingston's plan to appear as an ordinary wizard seemed to have worked as no one had pointed out the glamor he had placed on himself. His magical power remained hidden, for now.

He was later given a room and two sets of uniforms to wear along with a blue robe. Mr. Patrick had also informed him that he would be later handed a wand to help practice magic within school grounds. All the while, as Kingston sat across from Mr. Patrick in his office, Kingston had to keep himself from bursting out in laughter.

Not only had he successfully snuck into the school, he was now on his way to catch the culprit behind the dragon's kid-napping.

Kingston also wondered how Mr. Patrick would react if he knew Kingston really got his wand at the age of six.

Settling into his room after wasn't much trouble. Though it seemed quite odd to Mr. Patrick that Kingston hadn't packed up a lot of things, Ms.Hats had informed Mr. Patrick that Kingston was an orphan who didn't have much, making Mr. Patrick's fears give way to pity.

"You can decide the classes you'd wish to attend tomorrow from this list. I'd sug-gest you take your time to rest since you came all the way by yourself," Mr. Patrick suggested. He handed him a scroll right as Kingston was about to leave the office that was filled with wizard items all over, ranging from elixirs on the shelves, to maps, herbs, and rare items. It was both a thrilling and uncanny sight.

Kingston shook his head kindly at Mr. Patrick.

"I'm eager to learn, Mr. Patrick, so if no one minds, I'll be attending classes right off the bat," Kingston said with a grin.

The faster he could get to the root of who kidnapped the dragon, the better.

Mr. Patrick exhaled deeply as he rubbed his stubble beard. In a way, the old wizard reminded him of old man Ray.

"Alright," Mr. Patrick wished him luck, re-minding him to come over if Kingston ever needed someone to talk to.

Luckily for Kingston, he didn't have much of a problem locating his room as he nav-igated through turns, hallways, and the moving stairs that almost crept Kingston out for a moment. He avoided making eye contact with other students looking his way curiously as he made it to his room.

The room came open on its own as it had a magic sensor which could sense a per-son's presence. The space also seemed big enough for five people, but Kingston only noticed a bed which he assumed was his.

"It's quite the room, isn't it?" Kingston

turned his head to ask Crowly but smiled when he noticed Crowly had slept off amidst the entire conversation with Mr. Patrick.

And soon, after dropping his things off, he joined Crowly to finally rest for the day.

The next day, Kingston was harshly woken up to the sound of bells. His ears felt like they could burst at any moment as he jumped out of the bed in fright. The sound also alarmed Crowly, who was now flying all over the room.

When Kingston realized it was simply the school bell, he calmed down a bit. Of course, they would be woken up by some kind of alarm.

"Relax, Crowly. It's just the bell," Kingston said with a sigh, glad that he didn't have a roommate to witness his and Crowly's strange conduct.

Kingston had never been to a boarding school before, and back at his hometown, only the kids of the famous wizards could afford to go to schools such as this. Kingston only hoped that his secret of not being a real student would not be blown by his doings.

Upon hearing it was simply a bell, Crowly relaxed even with his heart still beating fast. He watched as Kingston jumped off the bed, grabbing the scroll Mr. Patrick had given him the day before.

"Hmm," Kingston hummed as he looked

over the list of classes he could choose from to attend for the day. A particular one caught his eye.

It was the magical beast finder class.

It was the perfect class for looking into both students, teachers, and getting tips on finding the dragon. But, it was set to take place in the afternoon. Meaning, Kingston had to attend two other classes before noon.

He thought of two other classes he would want to take and quickly began preparing for his first, 'broom riding,' which was to begin in an hour.

Thankfully each room had a bathroom in which Kingston had his bath and dressed up in the uniform Mr. Patrick had given to him.

Once he was done, Crowly hopped onto his shoulder.

"So, you've got a plan?" Crowly asked as Kingston made his way out of the room down the hallways. Kingston didn't really know much about the school's layout even though a map of the school was behind the scroll Mr. Patrick had given him. So he followed the other students closely as they made their way out of the boys' dorm.

"The plan is to act normal,"

Crowly snorted in reply. "Good luck with that, Kingston."

Kingston chuckled a bit, following the troops of students as they walked into another similar red-bricked building. And just as the student before him stepped into the revolving glass doors, Kingston grabbed onto the student's shoulder.

"Uh, excuse me?" He called out, his hands a bit shaky and as the person turned.

It was a girl.

And she looked about his age too. Her blonde wavy hair was covered by the drape of her blue, magic robe. Kingston saw that she held onto a scroll similar to his.

"Can I help you?" The girl asked, tilting her head slightly to the side. Her voice was a bit high and her blue eyes flickered from Kingston to Crowly who was tucked on his shoulder. She seemed to be a bit shy.

"Uh, I'm Kingston. I'm new here and I was hoping you could help me find the broom riding class? Mr. Patrick gave me a map but I'm pretty bad at reading maps." He lied through his teeth. But it wasn't like he could come entirely clean to a stranger he just met.

The curious girl grinned.

"Perfect. I'm Lisa and I'm pretty new too," She said, shifting out of the way as some students passed by and Crowly took the chance to whisper into King-ston's ear.

"Can we trust her?"

Kingston shrugged in reply just as Lisa grabbed hold of his hands and started to pull him forward, taking Kingston by surprise.

"Luckily for you, I happen to know every bit of this school, and your pet crow's pretty cute by the way." Her shyness melted as she inspected Crowly up and down.

Crowly blushed at Lisa's compliment but remained silent. He wasn't really sure he wanted people at the school knowing he could talk. Talking animals were still rare in the magical community.

"Thanks, his name's Crowly, by the way,"

Kingston answered on his behalf and started to follow Lisa who made a humming sound in response. As they walked, Lisa also told him that the broom riding class was held at the back of the school building, the field, as she called it.

Kingston had to stop himself from gasping at every single thing while they walked down the school halls. The ground was covered in marble, portraits of famous widely known wizards hung on the wall, students walked around with their pets, a few familiar to Crowly, and others really strange.

They finally got to the back of the building after passing through a fake wall. Lisa called it a shortcut as they didn't have to walk around the building. Kingston was met with the sight of a large green field with students already up on brooms and two adults watching them.

Upon hearing their footsteps, some of the students along with one of the adults turned, revealing a tall, lanky man whom Kingston assumed to be in his 30's. Unlike the other teacher beside him, he didn't have a magic robe on. He was dressed rather informally with his long black hair pulled into a ponytail.

"You're late again Lisa," The man scolded. Then, as his eyes flickered over to Kingston's, a frown graced his face, a frown that grew deeper the longer he stared at Kingston who had frozen in his steps.

There was something off about the man but Kingston could not place his finger on what it was.

"I assume you're new?" The man asked, now gaining the other teacher's notice. But Kingston stayed silent just as Lisa nudged him to say something.

The man's partner, a red-haired petite lady with round-rimmed glasses, had been talking with one of the students. Now, she turned with a hand on her hip, beckoning for both Kingston and Lisa to come closer. But Kingston felt stuck in place.

Maybe it was the strange man who seemed as though he could see right through Kingston's glamor. Or perhaps the students watching him. Kingston could not understand why his legs would not move.

Lisa seemed to notice this as she tugged him forward, to where the two adults were standing.

"Ahh, Lisa, the ill famed late-comer. And who might you be young one?" The lady asked, raising a brow.

To Kingston, she seemed kind and less scary. Her cheeks were a rosy pink, and Kingston felt a bit safe as he found the bravery to introduce himself.

"My name is Kingston. I just enrolled yesterday," Kingston said sheepishly, his words faltering when he noticed the man staring at Crowly.

He seemed to make Crowly nervous too because he slipped under Kingston's magic robe.

"Well, welcome to the broom riding class, Kingston. My name is Mrs. Aria and this is my partner, Mr. Dawson. We're both in charge of this class and the beast finder magic class."

Kingston nodded stiffly at her words, wanting to flee from their gaze as fast as he could. The odd feeling grew stronger the longer he remained with them.

"Great. Lisa here can show you the ropes and Mr. Dawson will be over to help you in a minute,"

Kingston opened his mouth to object to

Mrs. Aria about Mr. Dawson but she had already turned on her heel to attend to some of the other kids. Kingston felt the hair on his body rise as he could still feel Mr. Dawson's eyes on him. But Lisa was already dragging him to the other side of the field where other kids were awaiting their turn on the broom.

"Mrs. Aria says that we get our own broom based on our overall performance for the session," Lisa explained to him with glee, though her regards were on two students having problems with their brooms as they rose higher and higher.

One of the students, a boy, almost fell off, shaking up everyone as he could be badly injured from such a fall. Kingston stepped forward without thinking, his hands searching in his pockets for his wand. But Mr. Dawson came to the kid's rescue as he waved his wand in the air, a whirlwind went up to get the boy and got him back to the ground.

The two adults rushed over to the kid's side as soon as he landed with a soft thud on the ground, and Kingston watched Mr. Dawson as he attended to the blue-haired kid who was now crying.

When everything was sorted, it was now Kingston and Lisa's turn as they were the last in line.

Lisa handed Kingston a broom as he stepped forward into the spotlight. Lisa seemed excited as she grabbed the other broom, not bothering to listen to Mrs. Aria's mandates.

"Just let the broom lead you, Kingston. If you're able to control your magic flow, the broom will listen to you." Mrs. Aria whispered into his ear.

Kingston internally rolled his eyes but nodded nonetheless. He first rode a broomstick at seven. This was child's play to him but he couldn't have anyone finding out he knew too much. Mainly Mr. Dawson.

And so, as Mrs. Aria left his side, he sat on the long wooden broom, and inwardly let go of his magic control, letting his magic go haywire so that instead of flying normally like Lisa was, his broom started to move randomly. Up, down, left, right, it moved in a manner that made the kids watching scream out.

Kingston wanted to laugh out loud as he was clearly having fun at their scared faces and Mrs. Aria yelling at him to try and keep calm. She likely thought he was in danger. But he had everything under control.

Though, he hoped that Mr. Dawson, the strange man who was silently watching, didn't suspect him.

CHAPTER SEVEN

After his broom came crashing down, the entire class came rushing toward Kingston to find out if he was hurt.

Kingston couldn't be caught looking happy at the thrill he had just had. So, he pretended to be hurt. He even acted as if he was sad he could not control his broom.

"I tried but, it didn't work," he sulked,

making Mrs. Lisa wrap her arms over him to comfort him. He could feel Crowly underneath his cloak shaking his head at his act.

"It's alright. You have many more classes to get better," Mrs. Aria said to him right before she unwrapped her and held his shoulder firmly. With a nod from Kingston, she smiled sweetly.

As soon as she left to say something to Mr. Dawson, the other kids crowded around him.

"Were you scared?" a boy asked, and Kingston recognized him as the boy who fell off his broomstick earlier. He had odd blue hair and unlike others, his blue robe had quirky designs on it.

Kingston opened his mouth to say 'yes' but was cut short by a hug from Lisa who had stopped flying on her broom at the sight of her new friend almost having a bad fall on his first day.

The hug felt a bit weird to Kingston. Even more so because he didn't have any friends other than Crowly. It felt strange having people care so much about him.

"Thank goodness you're safe. That was a close call," Lisa said, and Kingston chuckled shyly.

The other kids kept bombarding Kingston with questions until he was saved by Mrs. Aria who came over to dismiss the class with Mr. Dawson by her side.

As Mrs. Aria encouraged the kids not to give up and practice harder, Kingston's eyes were firmly planted on Mr. Dawson who was silently standing beside her.

The man sure didn't talk a lot, adding to the bad feeling Kingston already had about him.

He and Mrs. Aria were also the two teachers in charge of the magical beast finder class, and Kingston knew there was no way sweet Mrs. Aria could be a suspect. But then again, Kingston knew better than to trust anyone just because of his feelings about them.

Right as Mrs. Aria finished with her speech, the two adults turned to leave, and the kids started to head to their next class.

Kingston took it as his chance to ask Lisa about the two teachers as they started to walk away from the field.

"Mr. Dawson seems pretty strange, don't you think?" Kingston blurted out as his hands searched his pockets for the scroll that had his next class on it.

"Mr. Dawson?" Lisa thought out loud with her lips pursed.

Kingston nodded as he turned his head a bit to look at her while they walked back into the school building through the fake wall. Crowly, who had been hiding under his cloak, now slipped out from underneath.

Hiding in there was confining for Crowly, and now that they were away from Mr. Dawson's creepy stare, Crowly could fly beside Kingston and his new friend Lisa.

"Well, to be honest, I think every teacher in this school is pretty odd," Lisa laughed and then continued in a sing-song voice.

"Though Teddy says Mr. Dawson has quite the strange liking to magical beasts. But I bet it's because that's basically his job."

Kingston now stopped in tracks in the hallway at her statement. Some students gave him quite the stare at his abrupt stop as the halls were quite busy with kids and teachers heading to their next class.

Some unruly students were also riding their brooms in the hallway causing a lot of racket. But nothing seemed more important to Kingston than the new information he just gathered.

"Everything alright, Kingston?" Lisa asked, worry evident in her blue eyes.

Crowly and Kingston traded glances before Kingston faked a laugh and resumed walking even though he didn't really know where he was headed. His next class was defensive magic, and he didn't think there was anything he didn't already know about the subject.

Lisa sighed, "Great, well, I have defensive magic next so-"

"What are the chances," Kingston cut in on her. He needed Lisa around both as a friend and as an informant, so it was perfect for him that they were sharing the same classes. "I've got that class too."

And with a grin, Kingston locked his arms over Lisa who was left speechless by every single thing he did.

'He's quite the outgoing kid,' she said to herself and began leading him to the next class with Crowly flying beside them, looking around for anything that looked strange other than the usual ruckus going on.

Their next class, Defensive Magic, was supervised by an old wizard, and Kingston could recognize some familiar faces of some kids from the broom riding class. One kid with the blue mop-like hair came up to him and Lisa, introducing himself as Teddy, the kid Lisa had spoken about before.

And though all fingers were starting to point to Mr. Dawson, Kingston still kept a keen eye on the wizard teaching them about defensive spells.

The class was held in a classroom with seats and tables, unlike the broom riding class which had been in the open field. The sitting made Kingston feel a bit cramped with all the kids around, and the fact that the teacher in charge, Mr. Beardman, didn't like pets.

So Crowly and a bunch of other pets

were kept in the pets' area while the kids were left to sit alone in his boring class.

Kingston didn't like to brag, but he was pretty sure that the teacher got some of the spell chants and words wrong, and since it wasn't a trial class, Mr. Beardman couldn't be called out.

And so, Kingston had to spend the next hour looking at the wall clock that seemed to tick ever so slowly.

Finally, after an hour of tuning out Mr. Beardman's slow, robotic voice, it was finally time for his last class of the day.

The class where he could look into both Mr. Dawson and Mrs. Aria better.

Kingston, Lisa, and their new friend Teddy

now walked down to the Magical Beast Finder class together. Like Kingston, Teddy had a pet sparrow who followed him around. Though unlike Crowly, Teddy's pet, Candice, couldn't talk. Kingston could tell that much by simply looking at the sparrow which flew over to Crowly's side and wouldn't stop bugging him.

"You definitely seemed scared this morning at the broom riding class, but don't beat yourself up about it Kingston, I understand," Teddy told Kingston with a small smile as he patted his back in a kind manner.

Kingston furrowed his brow at the movement, not knowing whether to take Teddy's hands off from his shoulder as they walked side by side.

"Uh, Thanks," Kingston said softly, his eyes on Teddy's hands that now remained wrapped around Kingston's shoulders.

Kingston decided not to make too much of a fuss about it as his eyes roamed the hallway that was starting to become devoid of students. It still felt like a dream to be in a school with real students and teachers.

The thrill of and happiness that had dulled in Mr. Beardman's class returned, and soon, Kingston felt at ease with Teddy's arms over his shoulder. Teddy began to fill the other two in on what their next class might be about, while Lisa stepped ahead of them to lead and hasten them up.

They finally arrived at the Magical Beast Finder class that was held in a large hall. It kind of reminded Kingston of his hometown's magical library except that this hall didn't have any books or any other thing except for a few tonics and fake wands lying on a large brown table.

Luckily for the three kids, they weren't too late as a few others stepped in after them. Crowly, not wanting to be stared at by Mr. Dawson who was attending to the students, slipped into Crowly's cloak pocket.

"Alright kids, gather up," Mr. Dawson

clapped his hands in the air, motioning to the other few students like Kingston and his friends who were by the hall's entrance.

Mrs. Aria seemed to be busy adding more magical tonics to the desk which the students had now gathered. And with a sharp intake of air, Kingston followed his two new friends who walked up to where the two adults were.

'This is it,' Kingston said to himself.

Kingston made sure to stand where he could clearly see the two teachers by the far end of the large table.

Mrs. Aria first welcomed the class with her usual sweet smile.

"In today's class, we're going to learn about habitats where rare magical beasts live. Beasts like Griffins," At the mention of Griffins, the students gasped and Mrs. Aria chuckled before she kept on.

"Fairies,"

Another series of gasps came from the children.

"And," Mrs. Aria made a fake drumming sound. "Our school's mascot. Dragons."

At the mention of dragons, Kingston leaned in closer, almost pushing aside the kid who stood beside him. Mr. Dawson joined Mrs. Aria, picking up a flask filled with a shiny powder Kingston knew to be fairy dust.

"Magical creatures tend to have unique traits, odd outward aspects, and powers. For example, fairies can be found simply by the golden color of their pixie dust." Mr. Dawson's loud voice rang out in the hall, and while the other kids watched him in awe as he opened up the bottle and dumped it in the air, Kingston felt his heart beating rapidly.

Could Mr. Dawson really be the culprit?

If he wasn't, how then did he get his hands on fairy dust?

As though sensing his question, Mr. Dawson, placing the bottle back on the table, pointed at Mrs. Aria who handed him another dull flask.

"Mrs. Aria over here happens to be in charge of gathering all these samples which help us in understanding the creatures. I too am equipped with the knowledge on how to find them."

Kingston's brows raked at the statement. Did that mean they were working together? But Kingston only found one footprint along with the dragons.

Who was it really between Mr. Dawson and Mrs. Aria?

Mr. Dawson resumed showing them other things, like the toenail of a griffin, the feathers of a rare species of magical bird, the blue scales of a dragon which he claimed had been in the school for years as Dragons no longer existed.

The more Mr. Dawson spoke, the more confused Kingston got, and by the end of the class, Kingston felt lost. His shoulders dropped in defeat as the crowd which had gathered around the two adults started to disperse. Mrs. Aria wished everyone a good day.

Perhaps he was blinded by suspecting the wrong people? Even though they taught the class, it didn't really mean they were the dragon kidnappers.

But Kingston couldn't deny there was something off about Mr. Dawson.

"Everything alright new kid?"

At the sound of Mr. Dawson's voice from across the table, Kingston flinched. He had been so lost in his thoughts, he forgot Mr. Dawson was still in the room.

But just as Kingston decided to turn on his heel to leave, he realized how good of a chance he had. He could use the situation to gain the upperhand. Mr. Dawson seemed to be interested in him.

And so with his two heedless chattering friends behind him, Kingston asked the question that had been bugging him for a while.

"Uh-yes but I'm just a little curious about where you were able to find all these samples from. If the creatures are rare I assumed it would be hard to find them?"

There was a evident shift in Mr. Dawson's

demeanor which caused chills to run down Kingston's spine. But Mr. Dawson quickly masked his anger at the question with a smile.

"Well kid, if I must confess, I got all these from a friend. But don't tell anyone. I can't have the other children thinking I'm a quack."

A lie.

Kingston could see right through Mr. Dawson's lie. But still Kingston thanked him before turning to leave, grabbing Lisa and Teddy who were both completely heedless to everything happening.

"Whoa, Kingston," Teddy laughed at Kingston's hurried steps out of the hall. But

the only thing Kingston could clearly remember was the dark look that crossed
Mr. Dawson's face at his question.

CHAPTER EIGHT

Three days passed with Kingston posing as a student. Three days of Kingston thinking and thinking with Crowly on what his next move would be. Crowly said the night before that they should do a strict scanning of both Mrs. Aria and Mr. Dawson, but Kingston had no idea where to start.

In fact, since he arrived at the school,

Lisa and Teddy had been his guides, leading him basically everywhere. But he knew there was no way he could tell them about the dragon and the suspects he had in mind yet.

"Hmmm," Kingston realized that he had to follow Mrs. Aria or Mr. Dawson after their broom riding class. If he did this, he would not need to know where to begin his search.

Once the class was over and they all met up in front of Kingston's locker to talk, Kingston came up with a lame excuse to Lisa and Teddy as to why he couldn't join them for lunch. Slowly, they went on without him, leaving Kingston and Crowly who had been perched on his shoulder.

"Is the coast clear, Crowly?" Kingston asked as he grabbed onto his wand from his robe pockets. After taking a quick look around, Crowly replied with a 'yes.'

With Crowly's reply, Kingston waved his wand in the air.

"Trail, trails. Reveal yourself."

While in the broom riding class, Kingston had quietly cast a trailing spell on Mr. Dawson. So now, the blue string of thread flowing down the hallway to another part of the building was the trail on which Mr. Dawson had left behind.

Kingston gave Crowly a quick nod before he began following the thread, passing busy classrooms, offices, until the trail stopped right in front of a closed office, the thread vanishing into thin air.

From the large pane windows, Kingston could see Mr. Dawson on the phone with someone and another empty desk across from his, which Kingston concluded belonged to Mrs. Aria.

To avoid being seen, Kingston quickly hid behind a large pillar. But from his position, he could not hear anything.

"I think I might have to cast another spell to listen in on Mr. Dawson," Kingston whispered, holding onto the pillar. It was the only thing saving him from being caught spying by Mr. Dawson or anyone passing by.

"But it's too risky, Kingston," Crowly whispered back, twisting his head to check if anyone was around the corner.

Kingston sighed. He had to at least have an idea as to what Mr. Dawson was saying. It could help in his finding of the dragon. Kingston thought it was worth the risk.

Without talking to Crowly, Kingston flashed out his wand, his head peeking out from beyond the pillar as he whispered the words.

"Listen, hear, listen in to the words behind that-"

Kingston quickly hid his head behind the pillar with his heart beating hard as he had been almost caught by Mr. Dawson who suddenly turned his head Kingston's way.

It was as though Mr. Dawson could feel Kingston's powerful magic and turned to check where such magic was coming from.

"I told you it was too dangerous," Crowly scolded Kingston and then quickly urged Kingston to run as he could hear shuffling of feet from Mr. Dawson's office.

With his heart pumping quickly, Kingston quietly slipped away from behind the pillar, running down the hall until he locked himself inside the bathroom.

Kingston had assumed that his powerful magic couldn't be traced since he cast an glamor spell on himself. But he was wrong. If he hadn't listened to Crowly and run in time, his ordinary wizard cover would've been blown.

But it wasn't all bad for Kingston. At least now, he knew where Mr. Dawson's office was and he could go ahead with his nighttime spying plan.

In Kingston's eyes, the rest of the day passed in a blur with his mind only thinking of what the night had in store for him and Crowly. He couldn't even have time to listen in to Lisa and Teddy who bickered back and forth about the silliest of things.

Though Kingston wasn't annoyed at them being around him, in truth, he had started to get fond of them. He knew that it was only a matter of time before he would have to leave them.

But for the meantime, he had to gather as much info as he could about the two magical beast finder teachers.

By nighttime, Kingston had cast an invisibility spell on himself and slipped out of the boys' dorm. His magic was strong enough to last him until he reached the school building before the magic's effect ran out.

Dressed in good clothes, Kingston draped the hood of his sweater over his curly hair to help hide himself before he slipped into the school building.

A cold chill passed through the windows as soon as Kingston stepped in, causing both he and Crowly to shiver at the sudden feel of coldness. The strong light of the moon coming from the windows didn't help either as it gave the school building a rather haunting look with the shadow of the trees looking like giant monsters.

"Surely you're not scared, Crowly?" Kingston teased with a laugh as he started to walk forward, swinging his arms and legs. Crowly rolled his eyes, rumbling out a reply before noticing a red straight line which Kingston was about to walk past.

The line looked quite odd to Crowly who narrowed his eyes. Kingston seemed too busy teasing Crowly to notice. It wasn't until Kingston neared the line that Crowly realized what it meant.

"No, Kingston, it's a trap."

But it was already too late because Kingston had just stepped on the line, and out
of nowhere, flying arrows directed at
both Kingston and Crowly came charging
towards them.

Kingston acted quickly as he grabbed
Crowly by his wings, ducking and rolling
out of the arrows' way. But it wasn't over
because dodging the arrows only caused
Kingston to step on another one of the
red lines.

In fact, it was at that moment Kingston
noticed the red lines and that they were
at every step of the way, with each line

bringing a new trap they had to evade.

The ceiling above Kingston opened up, and before Kingston had the time to react, he was suddenly surrounded by iron bars that locked him in. Only Crowly had the opportunity to escape.

Kingston rolled his eyes at the simplicity of the traps the school had set in place to catch intruders. Honestly, an alarm going off would have been better.

With the wave of his wand, Kingston was able to make himself as skinny as a pencil and slip through the cage that immediately retracted upon his absence in it.

Kingston knew that he couldn't waste more time with the traps. So he tapped on his wand, causing the magical wooden stick to transform into a long broom.

"Hop on, Crowly, we're going to fly all the way to Mr. Dawson's office."

At Kingston's words, Crowly flew back to his position on Kingston's shoulder just as Kingston hopped on his wand, now turned flying broom that flew him across the entrance marked with visible red lines.

If the lines were close to his head, Kingston ducked while on the broom, and if the lines were a bit above the ground, the broom flew higher all the way until they made it to the front of Mr. Dawson's office.

With a tired sigh, and his breath coming out unevenly, Kingston jumped off from the broom that transformed back into the wand he always carried with him.

"I guess this is it," Kingston remarked, carefully stepping closer to the door of the office and checking around for traps.

"So, what's the plan other than the both of us snooping around?" Crowly asked just as Kingston stretched out his hands to open the door.

Kingston shrugged, a bit unsure. "I'm pretty sure it's Mr. Dawson. I mean, he lied when I asked him about where he got those samples from so-"

"But there's Mrs. Aria too," Crowly re-minded Kingston with a stern gaze. "We can't just cancel her out. Besides, if I re-member correctly, she's the one with more knowledge about the magical beasts."

Kingston sighed. Crowly was always right. At first, Kingston had decided on only snoop around Mr. Dawson's things, but now, Mrs. Aria had to be checked too.

"Alright then, you check Mrs. Aria's things, and I'll check Mr. Dawson."

Crowly agreed with a nod, and after clos-ing his eyes and taking a large whiff of air, Kingston muttered some magic words with his wand that got the large office door open.

The door made a scary creaking sound as it came open, revealing the office Mr. Dawson and Mrs. Aria shared.

The lights were turned off, and the only help for visibility they got was from the moon, which was now beginning to hide beneath the clouds.

The room was quite small, with stacks of papers on each teacher's table along with familiar bottles on both their tables and a shelf that contained books, tonics, weird-looking artifacts, and the like.

Kingston remembered where he had seen Mr. Dawson sitting earlier, and thus went over to his desk. Meanwhile, Crowly hopped off Kingston's shoulder and took the other desk.

Kingston's heart began thumping wildly as he started to check the files on Mr. Dawson's table. There were maps of different towns all over his table, but that couldn't be evidence against him as maps were also on the walls of the office.

There were reports about students, history of magical beasts, info about many monsters, but that was it. There was no information on the dragon. Kingston even went as far as opening each drawer, checking the shelves, everything but he could not find anything.

Did that mean he wrongly suspected Mr. Dawson of kidnapping the dragon?

Kingston could feel guilt in his stomach just at the thought of wrongly pinning the blame on Mr. Dawson simply because he semmed odd.

"Kingston, over here. You've got to see this."

Kingston's heart skipped a beat as he turned over to Mrs. Aria's desk. Even from across the room, he could see the family photo on her desk which had her, her husband, and two little kids.

The beautiful photo first caught his eyes before a paper which Crowly was holding up with his feet.

Kingston rushed over to grab the paper with his quivering hands, and his eyes skimmed through the paper that held Mrs. Aria's name and address, with a

handwritten letter requesting information on the location of the old dragon
nest.

"There's more," Crowly informed Kingston, a sad look on his face as he noticed
how Kingston's hands were shaking.

Kingston dropped the letter and stared
at the documents sprawled on Mrs. Aria's
table, all containing information about the
missing dragon.

And even if he didn't want to accept it,
everything now pointed to Mrs. Aria as
the dragon's kidnapper.

CHAPTER NINE

A wave of dizziness passed through Kingston's body the longer he stared at the documents on Mrs. Aria's desk, so with a sigh, Kingston walked over to settle down on her brown chair. It also didn't help that the room was beginning to get far too chilly for Kingston's liking.

It didn't just make any sense to Kingston.

Sure, he agreed not to overlook Mrs. Aria simply because she seemed sweet and kind, but Mr. Dawson had been acting off since the moment Kingston set his eyes on him.

"I know you don't want to believe it, Kingston, but it's obvious she's the one," his best friend softly said, gently landing on the desk with his wings spread out, pointing at the evidence.

But there was something wrong; Kingston could feel it in his bones.

"But you felt the creepiness from Mr. Dawson too, didn't you?" Kingston insisted with a deep frown, but Crowly shrugged in reply.

"He might be a creep but he's clean."

Kingston snorted, rolling his eyes. Now that they knew Mrs. Aria was the kidnapper, all that was left was to find out where the dragon was.

"Well, let's find more clues as to where the dragon is. We don't have much time to spend out here," Kingston, pinching the bridge of his nose, said, once again staring down at the document before him in disbelief.

And that's when Kingston saw it.

The ink on the letter Mrs. Aria had likely written seemed to blur, dancing atop the paper in an odd way. Kingston rubbed his eyes, tuning out the sound of Crowly opening up the drawers in Mrs. Aria's desk.

The paper went back to normal, but then a thought suddenly struck Kingston as he glanced back at the words on it.

What if there was something he could not see? Maybe there was something underneath the ink he had seen blurring away from the paper.

As Crowly complained about not finding any more clues, Kingston waved his wand in the air.

"Reveal, reveal, all that is hidden in this room."

Crowly turned his eyes away at the bright flash of light that surrounded the office, but Kingston's eyes remained stuck on the letter, whose words started to morph into something else to reveal the real words that had been on the letter.

Kingston could no longer see Mrs. Aria's name on the paper. Rather, Mr. Henry Dawson's name stared right back at Kingston.

"You've got to be kidding me," Kingston laughed.

Mr. Dawson had almost had him fooled. The man had cast a spell to turn things in his favor and put all the blame on Mrs. Aria, but now, Kingston could see beyond the tinted glass Mr. Dawson had cast upon the room.

"Something strange just appeared on Mr. Dawson's table," Crowly cried out, dumping a file he had suddenly found from across the room on Mrs. Aria's desk.

With a please grin, Kingston opened up the file to reveal documents whose contents included an application form for sales of magical creatures. This was an approved copy of the form from an illegal market known for selling off rare magical beasts.

Kingston also found another document regarding the black market. It's location as well as the evil wizards enlisted to keep out intruders at their upcoming market sales, and all the documents had Mr. Dawson's name underneath.

And the last piece of evidence Kingston needed was wrapped in a thin cloth, the blue scales of the dragon. The same one Mr. Dawson had shown them during the class.

Kingston was right all along.

Mr. Dawson was the culprit, and as a protective measure, he had put a spell making it so that all his documents held the name of poor, innocent Mrs. Aria.

"I can't believe it. Who knew he could do something so evil," Crowly gasped, and Kingston chuckled in reply.

It felt good knowing he was right and now, with the help of the dragon's scales, Kingston could locate and free the dragon before it got sold off to the black market. But, to attain his goal, Kingston knew he needed all the help he could get.

The next day, Kingston approached Lisa and Teddy by Lisa's locker with his mind entirely made up. He was going to tell them everything with the hope that none of them were secretly working for Mr. Dawson.

Lisa seemed to be saying something funny to Teddy as he threw his head back in laughter, and Kingston felt a little bad at the fact that for the past three days, his mind had been too occupied for him to fully spend time with them.

"Hey guys," Kingston said with a smile, gaining Lisa and Teddy's attention. At the sight of Kingston, Lisa quickly rushed over, grabbed his cloak, and pulled him close, locking her arms around his neck in a manner that made Kingston cry out in pain, while Crowly and Teddy watched, each stifling their laughter at the face Kingston was making.

"That is for suddenly ditching lunch yesterday to go do sketchy stuff," Lisa scolded, ruffling Kingston's curly hair before releasing him.

Kingston breathed out shakily as he tried to adjust his now rumpled cloak.

"I'm sorry, I, uh, had something going on," Kingston said just as the bell for their first class went off.

Lisa and Teddy traded a look at Kingston's words.

"Are you in any trouble?" Teddy asked, worried, in his usual soft voice. "If it's anything we can help you with, we definitely will. We are friends. Remember?"

Kingston gulped, lowering his gaze to the floor as he struggled with what to tell his friends.

He didn't think he could ever make friends aside from Crowly, but now, he had not just one but two new friends who were worried about him even though it had been barely a week since they met.

When Crowly saw that Kingston was still hesitating, he butted into the chat.

"It's top-secret information, so you both have to promise Kingston that you won't tell a soul about this."

Crowly must have forgotten the fact that both Lisa and Teddy didn't know he could talk because now, their eyes were wide as the moon, as each of them struggled to believe Crowly had just spoken.

Even Teddy's pet, Candice, seemed shocked too.

"You—you can talk?" Teddy asked, still very much blown away.

"Well, I guess it's part of the secrets Kingston would have shared with you if I didn't just butt in," Crowly chuckled shyly, flying behind Kingston, who rolled his eyes.

The hallway was quickly becoming empty with everyone rushing to class. They would be late, but Kingston needed to tell his friends.

With a deep sigh, Kingston finally spoke. "The truth is, I'm not really a true student of this school."

Lisa's brow furrowed as she gave Kingston's uniform a once-over, while Teddy couldn't wrap his head around Kingston's confession.

Kingston then sighed again before going into detail about his adventures as a wizard, the quest of finding the last dragon, and the identity of the teacher behind the kidnapping. He left out nothing, leaving his two new friends at a loss for words.

"You've got to be kidding me," Teddy whispered just as the shuffling of feet in the hallway caught their notice, and at the sight of their Principal, Mrs. Hats, the three friends along with Candice and Crowly rushed away to avoid getting caught.

"We'll talk about this after class by the janitor's closet," Lisa told Kingston right before they stepped in late for their Magical Potions class.

Throughout the class, Kingston couldn't stop the anxiety building in him at the thought that his friends probably didn't believe him. He wished he could use his magic to freeze time at the moment and get right back to talking with them. But he knew he had to be patient. He could feel their eyes on him from where they sat in the classroom, and it made him even more uneasy.

Right after the class, with Crowly on his shoulder, Kingston followed after Lisa and Teddy.

"Guys," Kingston called out as he trailed after them, afraid and worried that they had decided to ignore him or think of him as crazy.

Lisa turned, displaying with a wave of her hand to follow them. And with his heart still racing, he walked speedily by people to catch up with them until they made a turn into another empty hallway.

"This way," Teddy called out to him, and Kingston saw that Teddy had a wand, which he waved around before a door appeared.

"I thought you said to meet up at the Janitor's closet," Kingston breathed out heavily as he finally reached them. All the speed walking seemed to have worn him out.

Lisa shrugged. "We'll have more privacy here. Quick, come in before anyone sees us."

Lisa was the first to step in through the door, and Teddy followed right after with Candice flying in with him. Kingston warily walked through the door after sharing a look with Crowly.

The door led them to a tiny room with cleaning equipment, which made Kingston frown a bit. "Isn't this the janitor's closet?"

"Well, yes," Lisa said with a sigh. "But Teddy's pretty good at teleportation spells. It's safer to use this method to avoid suspicions."

Kingston nodded in understanding before an awkward silence settled in the air around them. No one seemed to want to say anything. It wasn't that Lisa and Teddy hated Kingston for all the secrets he kept from them; it was more of them being shocked about Mr. Dawson being some kind of villain. And they didn't even know dragons still existed.

Sure, he was weird and seemed a bit sketchy, but still.

"I know my story must've sounded crazy," Kingston finally broke the silence by saying. "But I need help. This isn't something I can do alone."

"He's right. We really do need help," Crowly added, hopping off Kingston's shoulder so the other two could see him properly.

Lisa and Teddy traded troubled looks before Lisa gave in with a sigh.

"Alright. What can we do?"

Teddy nodded along. "Yeah, Kingston,

though to be honest it seems odd that Mr. Dawson would kidnap a dragon and want to sell it off. But you're our friend. We'll help the best way we can."

Kingston breathed out in relief, his heart feeling warm at the fact that even though there wasn't proof to back up his story, his friends still wanted to help out.

"Thanks, guys."

"It's no problem, but I still can't get over the fact that Crowly talks," Teddy commented, earning a whack on the head from Lisa who rolled her eyes after and folded her arms. That should have been the least surprising thing that they learned.

"So any ideas?" She asked. If they were going to rescue the dragon, they needed information on where to find it, and any magical items or spells they could use to face off against Mr. Dawson.

Though Kingston had claimed to be a genius, Lisa still knew it would be hard to free the dragon alone from wherever it was being held.

"Teddy and I will get more help as well as spells and items we can use against Mr. Dawson. Also, one of us will have to stall Mr. Dawson a bit so we don't get busted while trying to free the dragon," Lisa said, her eyes going back and forth between each boy.

"I'll do it. I'm a crow, so it will be less sus-pect if I'm the one stalling him," Crowly chipped in, and Kingston frowned. He didn't like the idea of Crowly being away from him.

"But that's too dangerous, Crowly. Be-sides—"

"I don't want to hear it, Kingston. I have to help," Crowly stated, his beak puck-ered in stubbornness.

Kingston sighed, grumbling the words, "Fine, do whatever you want."

"Well, since that's settled, when do you plan on starting the operation?" Teddy asked, tucking back his wand he had been holding out the entire time back into the pocket of his robe.

According to the documents Kingston found, Mr. Dawson seemed to have planned to sell off the dragon the next weekend. So, Kingston would have to use the dragon's scales to find its location and rescue it before it was too late.

Meaning, they had to rescue the dragon by the weekend.

"In two days. We begin our mission to find the dragon."

CHAPTER TEN

For the next two days, Lisa and Teddy gathered as many defensive supplies as they could to help with the quest. They payed more attention in their defensive magic class, and Kingston, who didn't particularly like how the teacher taught, showed them a few tricks that could come in handy in case they were to encounter Mr. Dawson during the rescue.

Though Crowly was supposed to keep him

busy by distracting him, Kingston knew they had to be prepared for the worst.

Lisa and Teddy also snuck out three magic flying brooms from the school's equipment room. Though it was against school rules and clearly bound to put them in trouble if they were to wind up getting caught.

Finally, the day had arrived for them to free the dragon from wherever Mr. Dawson had kept it locked up.

The activities of the weekend passed in a blur for the three children as their hearts nervously got ready for the quest they had planned.

For the past two days, Kingston had been

carefully watching Mr. Dawson's every movement. The young wizard knew the time he always retreated to his private room at the teacher's dorms.

Since Kingston had no idea which room belonged to Mr. Dawson, he relied on the scales which he had taken from the office to lead him.

The chattering voices of students from their dorms that evening caused Lisa and Teddy to shiver in slight fear as they all met up outside of the Boys' dorm, as Kingston had instructed them the day before.

Teddy and Candace held up a big bag, containing all the items and supplies they had been able to get.

While waiting for Kingston to arrive, they dodged the odd stares from students passing by the dorm. They looked pretty suspect with the way they also kept looking around for Kingston. When he finally arrived with Crowly trailing behind him, dressed in his homemade brownish-red robe, Lisa and Teddy breathed out in relief.

The sun had now totally vanished behind the clouds, with the sky darkening by the second.

It was the perfect time.

"Let's go, guys, we don't have that much time on our hands," Kingston instructed his friends. With a shared nod between the three of them, they began walking down the path that led to the teacher's dorms.

They tiptoed whenever a teacher sounded close by, and whenever Kingston sighted one, he quickly cast an invisibility spell on them, though it couldn't last quite as long as it would if he were the only one.

The old him would have felt working with anyone other than Crowly tiring, but oddly enough, Kingston loved the thrill of fear and excitement his new friends provided him as they trailed behind him.

The teachers' dorms were large, stretching from one end of the school surrounded by the large walls to the other end. The buildings were also old-looking,

with vines sprouting out from each corner, leaving the buildings looking haunted.

Teddy shuddered in fear as they crouched
behind one of the pillars supporting the
buildings to avoid being seen.

"So what now? How do we find the
dragon?" Lisa whispered, her eyes all
over the place in search of any incoming
person.

Kingston checked for the dragon's scales
from his cloak's pocket and flashed it in
front of his friends.

"A tracking spell," he told them before
bringing out his wand and chanting the
words, "Track, track, track these scales!"
Kingston said, hoping this would lead

them to the dragon.

A blue trail of shimmering light came before them, and his two friends gasped in awe.

By now, they knew Kingston was quite the unique wizard. But his show of advanced spells caught them off guard.

Checking that the coast was clear, Kingston, in a crouched position, began to tiptoe forward as fast as he could, beckoning Lisa and Teddy to follow him.

The trail led them into one of the Quarters situated at the far end, and it seemed luck was on their side as no one seemed to be roaming around at the time.

When they got to the front of the building Kingston assumed Mr. Dawson resided in, he turned to Crowly.

"Are you sure you want to do this? You can join us inside instead of trying to put yourself in danger,"

Kingston still wasn't happy about the idea of Crowly acting alone, and so he hoped that he could try to change Crowly's mind one last time, but Crowly wasn't having it. He stubbornly crossed his wing arms together, his face turned away from Kingston.

Kingston sighed, and before he could open his mouth to say anything else, Lisa placed a hand on his shoulder to draw his gazed.

"We don't have much time, Kingston. Just trust him, he'll be fine," Lisa told him, her voice soft and easy.

With his shoulders slumped in defeat, Kingston realized he had no choice but to believe Crowly would be fine. And so after casting a spell to unlock Mr. Dawson's front door, Kingston and his two friends slipped in after wishing Crowly good luck.

Just like the outside of the dorms, the inside seemed like something out of an old fairy tale. The hallway following the front door seemed to be unending, with each corner lit by a gleaming orange light bulb.

On the walls, Kingston, Lisa, and Teddy

could make out the paintings and pictures of different types of dragons and other monsters, which added to Kingston's great dislike for Mr. Dawson.

"He really is a creep," Teddy remarked with a frown, following closely behind Lisa and Kingston ahead, the blue trail leading further into the building.

Kingston found it strange that he couldn't sense any traps put in place as they continued to take turns, pass by corridors, and locked rooms. There was something weird, and Kingston felt sad at the fact that Crowly wasn't beside him to share his advice. And though Teddy's pet sparrow hovered around them, Kingston couldn't see her as anything other than a

pet, though she was pretty cool sometimes.

The young wizard blew out yet another
sigh, hoping they could quickly find the
dragon as soon as possible and get on
with their lives.

Kingston's brow furrowed when he noticed the trail leading them up a flight of
stairs, and he turned to remind his com-
rades of their safety. He knew it was a
lot for them doing so much for him, and
he knew he would do everything to keep
them safe.

In fact, if they chose to leave him out of
fear at that moment, he wouldn't hold it
against them, even for a moment.

Their nice smiles back at him caused his eyes to widen a bit. Lisa flashed her wand before using it to poke him in the back, as if asking him to move forward. With a soft laugh leaving his mouth, Kingston went up the stairs until the blue magic trail finally stopped in front of a large metallic door. It was heavily bound with chains and locks.

"Think we found it," Lisa commented and then snorted after. "I mean, he made it so clear he's hiding something behind the door."

Teddy nudged her. "You should not be talking so loudly. What if he hears you?"

Lisa rolled her eyes before turning her

gaze to Kingston, who was carefully looking at the door to check for any trace of
traps. When he found none, he turned to
give Lisa a chance to open the door.

"It's safe to break in," He said, "Remember what I showed you."

Lisa grinned, with a quick nod, fishing out
her wand from the pockets of her robe
and waving it around the air like Kingston
had shown her a day back.

"Open, open, let us in without a sound."

The chains binding the metallic door quietly broke free as well as the locks, and
without so much as a sound, the huge
doors came open revealing an empty
large room.

Well, empty apart from the huge cage sitting in its center with a familiar animal trapped in it which made the children gasp.

"Is-Is that really a dragon?" Teddy pushed past Kingston and Lisa, dropping off the bag he had been holding to the ground.

Teddy was far too excited to notice the piece of string lined across the room waiting to be stepped upon. And in fact, the other two kids were too busy gawking at the hunched over gleaming blue dragon to realize the trap Teddy had walked into.

Candice began to squawk out in alarm, but it was already too late as Teddy tripped over the string, thereby tugging it and unleashing a horde of bats appearing from thin air.

Kingston resisted the urge to smack himself on the face as he watched Lisa trying to quickly help Teddy up, while also swatting away the bats flying around and cornering them. It felt as though the bats were clawing at their faces, and they each tore out terrified screams, frantically waving their hands.

Kingston knew he had to act fast to avoid getting caught, and the sounds of his friends screaming didn't sit well with him either. He wondered how Crowly was faring outside all on his own. With a sigh, Kingston, while still standing outside the room, waved his wand, shouting the words, "Bats, Bats, go away."

He quickly ducked as a few came charging his way harshly before vanishing into thin air, and one by one, all the bats were gone, leaving behind not even a wing.

"Whew," Kingston commented, walking into the room and past a shaken Teddy and Lisa hunched over with their hands over their heads.

"It's ok, guys," He said to them. "They're all gone now."

Upon closer view, Kingston could now clearly see the dragon whose skinny pupils were now fixated on him, the person who had halted it from its nap.

The dragon was beautiful.

And though trapped in a large cage protected by strong magic, Kingston could
still feel its power. Its eyes quietly stud-
ied Kingston, who slowly inched forward
in order not to scare it.

"We're not here to hurt you," Kingston
promised, and the dragon's gaze moved
to the other children, still trying to regain
their confidence.

The dragon didn't trust them yet, so with
a loud growl, it moved away from Kingston and away from the light from the
moon, allowing it to blend in with the
darkness.

It didn't trust humans. With good reason
considering what had happened so far.

Kingston sighed. He knew that if the dragon were to trust him, he'd be able to set it free quickly. But then again, the spell and enchantment cast on the cage was far more complex than he had ever seen. Still, Kingston was determined to set it free.

"You'll be free, I promise," Kingston said to the dragon before running over to meet his friends.

"Guys. I need both of you to pull yourselves together. I know you're scared, and I wish I didn't have to put you through all these," Kingston took a sharp breath, and then continued to speak in a rush. Now that the alarm had gone off, he wondered how long Crowly could distract Mr.

Dawson.

"There's been a change of plans. Mr. Dawson might be back home at any moment, and I'll need the both of you to hold him off while I focus on freeing the dragon."

Teddy, who was still a bit shaken by everything happening so quickly, shot up his head, getting more terrified by the second. "What? No Kingston, we can't face him alone. Not now"

"Yes, you can. I won't take long, I promise. Please-"

"It's ok, Kingston. Just go," Lisa shoved him away before grabbing Teddy up and calming him down, whilst Kingston, with one last look at his friends, started to cast out different spells in a bid to free the dragon.

With each failed spell, sweat poured out from Kingston's forehead.

Seconds went by, turning to minutes, and just when it seemed like the powerful magic surrounding the cage had lessened, a familiar chilling voice caused Kingston and his friends to go cold.

"Well, well, well. Look what we have here."

CHAPTER ELEVEN

Kingston knew Crowly's plan had failed the moment he sighted Mr. Dawson from a distance, dressed in his normal clothes. The man had simply shoved Crowly aside with his wand before Crowly could even attempt to distract him.

And so, filled with panic for his best friend, Crowly followed the evil wizard into the dorms, pecking and cawing at him at every turn. But Mr. Dawson simply ignored him.

It was obvious the man had more pressing problems to attend to.

Problems like his secret room being invaded. He had been alerted by one of the bats when the string was pulled, and so he rushed over in haste to stop the intruder.

Though Mr. Dawson could only picture one familiar face in his head.

So then, rather than being surprised to see Kingston at the center of his secret room, trying to free his most prized trophy, he simply snickered knowing his hunch about Kingston was proven true.

Right from the day the boy had oddly enrolled in the school, Mr. Dawson knew
there was something odd about him. And
now, it seemed the feeling was mutual.

Lisa and Teddy, who had promised Kingston to hold off Mr. Dawson, got out
their wands, even while knowing they
could not hope to beat him.

"Keep trying to get it out, Kingston," Lisa
yelled out to the young wizard, who was
suddenly torn between helping his friends
and setting the dragon free.

Mr. Dawson laughed grimly at the cheap
display of friendship between them. He
always found children rather silly.

There was no way anyone would ruin his

plans. Especially seeing as how he had gone through all the trouble of kidnapping the dragon. And he even planned to pin all the blame on Mrs. Aria to avoid any punishment. The payday for selling such a rare and powerful monster was going to be life changing. And he wasn't going to let three meddling children get in the way of that.

"You kids will never understand how hard it is to be an adult. Judge me all you want, but I won't let you mess up everything!"

Suddenly filled with anger, Mr. Dawson flashed out his own wand, but Lisa beat him to casting a spell.

"Wind, come once, come twice, push out!" She said as she cast a spell to send him flying out of the room with a strong wind.

Mr. Dawson was more experienced but any wizard could be bested if they were taken by surprise. Unfortunately, Mr. Dawson would not be beaten that easily. He got up and charged at Lisa, this time with a spell of his own.

"Splash and gash!" Mr. Dawson said calmly, not taking Lisa very seriously. The spell created a blade of water with the sharpness of a sword.

Lisa made a protective shell out of her magic, but it crumbled at Mr. Dawson's spell. Lisa was pushed back on her bottom, rattled from the attack.

Teddy, seeing his friend hurt, rushed forward to help. He knew he was not much of a threat but at the very least, he could do some protective magic to help Lisa.

Meanwhile, Crowly, who had followed closely behind Mr. Dawson, slipped into the room and amidst the duel, found his best friend trying to get the dragon out.

Crowly knew he had to think fast. It didn't look like Lisa's magic was doing much against Mr. Dawson. And even though Teddy had now cast a similar spell, it wasn't long until Mr. Dawson would beat the both of them.

"Why don't you try a complex spell, Kingston? Just like you did in the forest. If it doesn't work, then we'll just have to fight him and get him to break the spell himself," Crowly advised before perching atop Kingston's shoulder.

Kingston bit down on his wobbling bottom lip. He was always considered a genius, but in reality, no one knew how hard it was for him to get a lot of things done. Magic was not simple. It took a lot of creativity and skill to do complex spells.

Not even his best friend, Crowly, understood that much. Though he was a brilliant kid, he wasn't perfect.

However, this didn't mean he wouldn't try his best. But what kind of complex spell would work? The magic prison seemed unbreakable.

"Think Kingston. Think." He said to him-self.

"If you can't break the spell trapping the dragon, why don't you make the dragon get around the spell somehow?" Crowly said, as if it made much sense.

But maybe Crowly was onto something. Kingston always trusted his friend's council. A spell that could make the dragon immune to the cage? What kind of spell would do that?

As Kingston thought about it more, the battle raged on between Lisa, Teddy, and Mr. Dawson.

Kingston could hear it but did not dare to look backward. For he knew, if he did, he would forget the dragon and join the fight.

"Thunder, stutter, clutter, and flutter!" Teddy and Lisa yelled out in unison. From out of nowhere, a thunder cloud popped up above Mr. Dawson. It rained down lightning upon him. But he was too quick, no longer caught off guard. He used his magic to double his speed.

"Speed, lead me to freedom!" He said calmly. This spell seemed to give him in-human speed.

He now was running and hopping off the walls at the speed of lightning, all while casting spells of his own. Water blades, wind, and more elemental attacks struck the duo, even though they tried to defend themselves with magic.

Kingston had to act fast. "Make the dragon immune to the spell..... that's it!!" Kingston realized. The spell was reacting to him, just like the defensive spells in the school. He thought about when he slipped out of the school traps, they retracted. They only trapped what they thought was there.

If he was to make the dragon invisible, even if for just a little while, the cage spell would retract. And the dragon could get free. Or at least, he hoped.

Casting an invisibility spell on something as big as a dragon would be hard, but Kingston got to work.

Kingston muttered a thanks to Crowly and after drawing in a sharp breath, yelled out a series of complex, jumbled words all sounding like gibberish to anyone not familiar with it. It hurt his head to even think so hard, and it felt like most of his magical energy was draining.

But, for a slight moment, the dragon turned invisible. And the caging spell retracted, leaving the dragon free. This was much to Kingston and the dragon's surprise, who had been watching everything from the shadows.It seemed like it realized that they, Kingston, Lisa, and Teddy, had all been trying their best to free it from the evil man who had caged it there.

With newfound vigor, the dragon came

forth from the shadows, towering over Kingston, who shrank back in fear.

"No!" Mr. Dawson thundered, his eyes wide in disbelief at the dragon basking underneath the moon's light. Its narrow eyes glared directly at the man.

The dragon's sudden, loud, and terrifying growl seemed to be directed solely towards Mr. Dawson. It was angry. The sound made Mr. Dawson stand as still as a rock.

Lisa, Teddy, and his sparrow, who had been watching everything unfold, all ran to Kingston, whose hands were gently petting the dragon to calm it down.

The dragon leaned its head toward Kingston and allowed for him and his friends to get on its back.

"But our supplies, they're right out the door," Teddy voiced out his worries. If anything were to happen, Teddy thought that they would need the items in the bags.

"He won't be shaken for long, Ted, just hop on," Kingston instructed before climbing atop the dragon's back.

Lisa soon followed, and with a sigh, Teddy, though a bit wary of the animal, jumped on its back behind Lisa with Candice snuggled into his pockets.

The dragon, with blistering speed, flew up

and broke through the windows above the room right as Mr. Dawson ran back into the room to stop them.

The children watched the glass fragments chatter around them, and like bits of glitter, they shone brightly due to the moon's light, which they reflected. Due to the dragon's rock-solid body and scales, none of the children got hurt in the process.

"I can't believe we did it," Lisa laughed out loud, her hair strands dancing about in the wind due to the force of the dragon's wings as they flew.

"For a second there, I thought we were doomed," Teddy blushed, pulling down the hood of his robe and allowing the wind to play around with his hair.

From their placement in the sky, they could see the school buildings, which suddenly seemed like ants to them. Kingston grinned in delight at the success of his plans. Never in his dreams did he think he'd be riding on a dragon and escaping a teacher.

But little did Kingston and his friends know, they had Mr. Dawson trailing behind them. After all, Mr. Dawson was a master of broom riding. He was the one that taught Lisa and Teddy.

It wasn't until Teddy turned back to look at the teacher's dorms that he saw a ball of fire headed their way.

"Kingston. Fire," Teddy yelled quickly, moving closer to Lisa who tore out a scream at the bright red ball headed their way.

The dragon quickly moved aside to avoid the fireball, but it kept following them. Not intending to stop until it hit its target. And so it crashed into the dragon's tail, knocking it off balance and almost causing the children, now screaming at the top of their lungs, to fall off.

Mr. Dawson laughed as he got ready to launch yet another attack.

"I'm not letting that dragon go," he roared out with an evil laugh as he rode his broom swiftly.

With no other choice, Kingston realized he had to step up.

"What do you think you're doing?" Lisa yelled out in fright, watching Kingston getting up from his seated position and trying to balance on the dragon's back as it flew.

"Saving us," Kingston yelled back in reply and then turned to Crowly, who was still hanging onto Kingston's shoulder for dear life.

"Ready, Crowly?" Kingston asked. But the look on Crowly's face revealed the answer. "Don't tell me you're scared."

Crowly snorted back a shallow face as a reply before Teddy yelled to alert them of another incoming fireball. But this time, a snowball, water blade, and even lightning bolts followed as well.

"Protect, select, let us be protected!" Kingston said.

Kingston and his friends, along with the dragon, were quickly encased in a bubble that bounced back the attacks once they collided with it, sending them back to the wizard who had cast them.

And while the Mr. Dawson struggled to evade his own attacks, Kingston cast yet another spell.

But unfortunately, Mr. Dawson knew quite a bit about defensive magic as well.

"Vanish. Banish. Now," the old man bellowed, and all of the spells went up like thin air.

"What now?" Crowly asked, truly worried about what would come next.

Lisa, Teddy, and Crowly all looked up at Kingston with fear in their eyes. Kingston knew this was the part where he was supposed to do something heroic, but he had no clue what to do. Mr. Dawson was relentless. He was not going to stop until he got the dragon back.

"I.... I don't know" Kingston pushed out, looking down and hanging on as best he could as the dragon still washed through the air.

"All of the world is but a cage," Mr. Dawson yelled as a magic wall suddenly came before them. It looked like it had the strength of a mighty castle. The dragon stopped just before hitting it. It now had no where to go. And neither did the group of friends trying to free the dragon.

"We have to fight!" Kingston told his friends with his wand at the ready.

"It's over Kingston! Give me the dragon. NOW! And I won't hurt you or the other children."

Kingston didn't even bother to consult his friends. He already knew the answer. They could never do such a thing. "Never Mr. Dawson. You'll have to fight us for him."

Mr. Dawson sighed. "It did not have to be this way, children. If only you had not been so sneaky, so vile!"

"You are one to talk," Lisa yapped back at him.

"Very well then. Do not say that I did not offer you a way out of..." But Mr. Dawson had made a vast mistake. He thought he could beat three children. He thought that was all he would have to battle. But no. The one he should have been worried about...

The dragon's spine began to glow with a hot red that made fire look dim in comparison. It drew in air that looked like smoke from how hot it had become.

"How could I have been so careless..."
Mr. Dawson gashed out just as the
dragon blasted a horrid wave of fire at
him. The size of it could only be compared
to the mountain tops and the biggest
oceans.

Mr. Dawson casted a protective spell
just in time, but the dragon's wrath was
too much for him. He flew backward, and
downward wildly until he was out of sight.

"Whoa," Lisa and Teddy gasped out. They
had expected a bit of trouble, but this
was on another level. They had never
seen a dragon before. And they had no
idea how powerful he was. It was like a
force of nature.

The fire soon vanished from sight, though

the dragon's power created thunder clouds in its wake.

"We're good to go, dragon. Let's go far away from here," Kingston said, settling back on the dragon's back and watching as students and teachers started to run out of their dorms at the sound of the dragon's breath.

The dragon growled softly in reply before increasing its speed and flying away from the school again.

"Dragon? I wonder if he has a real name? Or if we should give him one?" Crowly asked.

"Well he's blue, so maybe bluey? I mean, I think it's a pretty solid name. Right, guys?" Kingston turned to his two friends behind him for agreement, and they grinned at him.

"It's blue. So Bluey's good," Lisa gave a thumbs up, and Teddy followed with a quiet laugh and a nod of approval.

"You sure made some pretty great friends," Crowly remarked, looking into the clouds and the landscape of mountains and forest before them as the dragon moved through the air like a hot knife in butter.

"That, I did."

The dragon flew for what seemed like hours. The ride was smooth and the kids wondered if it would ever end.

Lisa and Teddy soon slept off during the ride and were jerked back awake as the dragon gently landed on the grounds of yet another ancient forest that even Kingston didn't know of.

Due to the knowledge of his birthplace by dozens of humans, there was no way Bluey could return home. And so he had to settle with a forest where he could feel almost no trace of humans.

"Thanks, Bluey," Kingston rubbed its head right as he hopped off the dragon's back, and it leaned into Kingston's touch. Its soft growl echoing in the thick forest.

"Where are we?" Teddy asked drowsily as he and Lisa took in their surroundings.

The trees around were tall and thick, almost covering the sight of the clouds above them.

"We're at Bluey's new home," Kingston replied, turning his head slightly to find Crowly snoring softly.

It seemed as though everyone needed some sleep. They had quite the day. The kids began to get off Bluey and land on the soft forest floor.

"I think it's safe out here." He told them, making himself cozy on the ground beside Bluey, who now had its head rested on the ground and its large wings drooped as well. The dragon was likely tired from the long trip.

It had been a while since the dragon had the chance to fly, and he was grateful to Kingston for saving him. He moved his head closer to Kingston, who chuckled at his friends falling right back asleep, and before long, he joined in too.

...

The next morning, it was finally time to say goodbye, especially seeing as the kids had to return to school to face the music of their deeds. They had hoped everything would go quietly, but Mr. Dawson had to ruin it all by deciding to cause trouble and engaging in a midair combat.

Kingston woke up to the smell of musty breath that caused his face to scrunch up, and his eyes opened to find Bluey breathing down on him.

The laughter of his friends pushed around him, and soon after, he joined them in laughing at himself.

After checking that the forest Bluey had landed in was safe enough, Kingston decided they didn't have much time left.

"I guess this is goodbye, Bluey," Kingston sadly said, feeling the hard texture of Bluey's scales underneath his palm.

The dragon bared its teeth in an attempt to smile. It seemed Bluey had been around humans long enough to pick up on what a smile was. But Kingston did not find it quite as cute as the dragon may have intended. In fact, it was rather scary.

Lisa and Teddy followed along in bidding their goodbye, right after carefully looking at the dragon, rubbing its head, playing with its tail, wings, and horns.

And as Bluey watched his new friends leave the forest, a happy tear slid down its eyes in appreciation.

Bluey knew never to forget Kingston, Crowly, and the others who had helped him.

CHAPTER TWELVE

The journey back to the wizard academy was quite hard for the young wizards, especially for Lisa and Teddy seeing as they weren't quite used to traveling with their two feet. Kingston proposed they ride on his magic broom but they thought it would be fun to undergo walking a great distance with their legs.

But, as the hours passed, with the sun starting to peek out from beneath the clouds, and pricking at their skin, they gave up and eventually caved into Kingston's idea of broom riding.

Kingston turned his wand into a broom long enough to accommodate the three of them. And though it wasn't as nice as how it felt flying on a dragon, it still served its purpose of taking them back to the school.

With each passing moment they got closer to the hills where the magical school was carefully hidden. Lisa and Teddy could feel their hearts thumping wildly in fear of what was coming.

They were in big trouble. And though Kingston was worried too, he wasn't quite as nervous because he was not a real student. But he could get into trouble for pretending to be one and putting his friends in danger.

The entire ride was quiet with each young wizard silently hoping things wouldn't turn out too bad.

Kingston thought it better to go through the gates. He did not want to further complicate things by making them look like hooligans.

Soon, they stopped in front of the large gates, the familiar guard which Kingston had met on his first day at the school welcomed them with a great frown on his bearded face. He hit his palms together and waved them in quite harshly. He, for sure, knew something and was not happy about it.

"Oh, you three are in big trouble,"

"We can explain, just let us see Mrs. Hats." Lisa stepped forward to say, blocking the guards view of Crowly slipping in through the gates.

The children knew that they needed proof to prove that Mr. Dawson had committed a grave act, and so beforehand, they had planned for Crowly to sneak back into Kingston's room at the dorm, and get all the documents showing Mr. Dawson's evil doings.

The guard bellowed with laughter. "Oh you'll definitely meet her and trust me.

She's pretty mad."

The children went stock-still at the guard's words. If things went south, they'd be the ones kicked out from the school and not the actual evil-doer. Mr. Dawson may even lie and say that he had been trying to stop them from escaping the school after doing something bad.

It was all up to Crowly at the moment to return as soon as possible with the proof they needed to put Mr. Dawson in jail.

As though each feeling the same way, the three kids shared looks of skittishness before following the guards in through the gates to Mrs. Hats office.

As they walked in, they could all feel the

number of eyes watching their every move as if they were criminals. It made Kingston feel bad for involving his friends in his plan. If it weren't for him, they would not be in such a bad state with the school.

"I'm sorry, guys. It's all my fault," Kingston muttered, drooping his head in shame as they trailed behind the guard.

"Stop it, Kingston. We're not mad at you. I'll admit I'm a bit scared, but that's it," Lisa admitted, locking her fingers with those of Kingston's and giving him a warm smile.

Teddy concurred with a nod. "It's not like you forced us to come with you, so it's okay."

Kingston could feel his eyes brimming with tears, but he refused to let them fall just yet. He knew he would have to do everything in his power to make sure his friends would not be punished.

"Thanks, guys," he smiled. "I won't let you down."

After trailing behind the guard on the empty hallway leading to Mrs. Hats' office, they finally arrived at the front of her large door. The kids traded nervous gazes as the guard softly knocked and then stepped into her office.

"It'll be fine. We'll be fine," Kingston said to them, and right on time, Crowly returned from Kingston's room with the documents and proof they had taken from

Mr. Dawson's room just as the guard returned.

The children let out a sigh of relief upon seeing Crowly and each muttered a 'thank you' underneath their breath.

"Good luck in bailing yourselves out of this," the guard remarked with a slight scowl on his face before ushering them into Mrs. Hats' office and leaving right after.

As the kids stepped into Mrs. Hats' office, they were first greeted with the stern, displeased look on her face, even as she towered over everyone in the room while seated. Then, they noticed Mr. Dawson seated across from her, rambling on about how he was trying to stop the kids from running away. He still had a bit of a hot tinge from the dragon's breath. He smelled like a pig roast. Mrs. Hats couldn't wrap her head around why Mr. Dawson ended up in such a state if he were telling the truth.

"I need answers, now!" Mrs. Hats ordered, her tone clipped. She was tired of hearing just half of the story.

Her words had been directed at the kids, who she had sensed without even looking their way.

Mr. Dawson turned, and upon seeing Kingston, began to yell out, "It's his fault. He's the mastermind behind everything. Don't you think it's a little strange? Just when he enrolled in the school, everything went sideways."

Kingston could feel cold sweat trailing down his forehead as Mrs. Hats' cold gaze met his eyes.

He wasn't guilty, but Mr. Dawson was right in an odd way. Kingston had been the one to instigate the problems in Mr. Dawson's life.

"We can explain, Mrs. Hats," Teddy, who usually hated being in the spotlight, stepped forward. He had his hands softly clasped behind his back before he pointed at Mr. Dawson, whose face was turning more and more red with each passing second.

"Mr. Dawson kidnapped the last dragon

from its habitat and planned to sell it at some shady market. Kingston caught on to his plans and stopped him-"

"Is that true, Mr. Dawson? You had a dragon trapped at this school?" Mrs. Hats now turned her gaze back to Mr. Dawson, whose hands were now shaking.

This gave the children more confidence, as it seemed Mrs. Hats believed them. But Mr. Dawson wasn't going to give up so easily. It was his word against theirs. And besides, he could still pin everything on Mrs. Aria if push came to shove. Or so he thought.

Yes, he was prepared for anything coming his way, but little did he know that Kingston and his friends were one step ahead.

239

Mr. Dawson faked a chuckle. "Oh, these kids, they come up with the craziest stories. But come to think of it, I do know Mrs. Aria had some weird hobbies-"

"Mrs. Aria did nothing wrong. I have proof," Kingston didn't allow Mr. Dawson to continue spewing his lies, and with a nod from Kingston, Crowly placed all the documents they had found in Mr. Dawson's office on Mrs. Hats' table.

Carefully, Mrs. Hats picked up the paper while Mr. Dawson remained in his seat with a huge grin on his face. He had used magic to have Mrs. Aria's name written on every document instead of his.

He won, and he would definitely make

sure Kingston and his friends were ex-
pelled, but Mr. Dawson found it strange
that the kids, instead of shaking in their
boots, were smiling right back at him as
though saying, "Think again."

"An underground market. Sales of rare
magical beasts. Really, Mr. Dawson?"

Mr. Dawson shrank back into his seat at
the look on Mrs. Hats' face before she
threw the documents his way, allowing
him to see his name on every document.
And before he had the time to cast a
spell, Mrs. Hats had beaten him to it by
calling out:

"GUARDS!"

They rushed in and grabbed Mr. Dawson

urgently. He tried to struggle a bit for show, but he knew it was no use. He did not want to become an outlaw, running from the magic police. So he gave in and allowed the guards to take him.

"Goodbye, Mr. Dawson. Have fun in jail," Lisa taunted with a grin as they all watched him get dragged off while yelling at the top of his voice.

They were now left with Mrs. Hats, who pinched the bridge of her nose with a sigh. The underground network had been exposed, and with the knowledge she now had, she thought someone needed to bring these people to justice. But that would be a problem for another time.

"Thank you, kids. That was very brave of

the three of you," she told them, the stern look on her face softening by the second and giving way to a smile.

Kingston let out a sigh of relief just as Lisa and Teddy pushed him forward.

"It was all him, Mrs. Hats. He's the one who did everything," Lisa said, wrapping her arm around his neck.

Mrs. Hats raised a brow. She had imagined Kingston as a troublemaker after last night's event and planned to suspend him. But she was suddenly seeing him in a new light.

"Is that so? Then you certainly deserve some praise."

Indeed, some praise would clear the

doubts the students had started to have about Kingston and his friends.

"Well, I don't think that'll be needed for me," Kingston scratched the back of his neck nervously. Everyone deserves to know the truth. The truth that he had been lying to everyone this whole time. Sure, he had his reasons. But a lie is a lie.

So Kingston took the chance to tell Mrs. Hats and his new friends the whole truth, and by the end of his reveal, the room was awkwardly silent.

"You're leaving?" Lisa was the first to break the silence by saying. Without meaning to, tears had already gathered in her eyes and were now streaming down her cheeks.

"But—you're a great student, Kingston. We'll have fun together," Teddy's choked-up voice said.

"That's right, Kingston," Mrs. Hats affirmed, rising from her seat. "I can excuse all of the chaos you caused yesterday, and besides, when everyone gets to hear the truth, you'll be a hero."

Kingston was surprised. He thought that they would all dislike him after learning the truth. But they did not. Even Ms. Hats wanted him to stay.

The offer was tempting, but that simply wasn't Kingston. He was a quester. He was a wandering wizard who just happened to drop by for a while. And as much as he loved his time at the school, he knew there were many more fun quests awaiting him.

With his head hung low, Kingston apologized. "I'm sorry, guys, but I just can't stay."

Lisa and Teddy had their eyes fixed on Kingston's form in shock. They had expected him to laugh it off as a joke, but he said nothing else.

The sound of Lisa's sobs filled the room as she hugged Kingston, with Teddy joining in soon after, and Kingston found himself crying along.

He knew he would miss them. He would miss school. His time at the school had been fun.

"Kids, huh?" Crowly remarked with a wistful smile as he flew right beside Mrs. Hats, who had been smiling at the children.

She turned to Crowly, a bit surprised at his words, but rather than asking any questions, she laughed softly, agreeing to his statement with a nod.

CHAPTER THIRTEEN

After breaking free from their group hug, Kingston told his new friends that he'd try to visit as often as he could. Though it didn't make them any less sad, it at least gave them a bit of hope that they'd see Kingston again.

Kingston even wished they could join him on his next quest. But unlike him, Teddy and Lisa couldn't just make decisions on a whim. And he was pretty sure Mrs. Hats wouldn't allow them to step foot outside the school any time soon.

"I promise to teach you as many magic tricks as you'd like when I come back," he told Lisa, whose eyes were puffy red and her cheeks reddened in embarrassment when Mrs. Hats, who had been watching them the entire time, handed her a tissue. Lisa hated people seeing her cry, and it was one of the few moments she allowed herself to cry in public.

On the other hand, Kingston promised to teach Teddy how to control his magic and ride a magic broom properly, seeing as Teddy still had quite some problem controlling his magic. It wasn't that Teddy wasn't talented already; he just had a few problems when it came to magic control.

The promises he made to them brought a smile to their faces, and once again, they shared a hug.

Though Kingston had told Mrs. Hats not to bother with the public praise, Kingston and his friends were hailed the next day as Mrs. Hats issued an emergency meeting with the entire school.

Kingston could hardly contain the bubbling feeling inside his chest at seeing everyone stand and clap for him and his friends.

He liked it. The feeling of being a hero was something he had always aimed for, and he was sure that if he were to remain at the school, he'd be treated like a celebrity by both students and teachers.

Some were already staring at him like one, so much so he had to bow his head and cover his face with his hood while exiting the hall. In contrast to Kingston and Teddy acting all shy, Lisa enjoyed every bit of being the center of the students' gaze.

"As I said, Kingston, you and your pet crow are always welcome back here anytime. It's all up to you," Mrs. Hats reminded the young wizard as she placed both hands on his shoulders. Her eyes flickering from those of Kingston's to Crowly who stood at his usual spot on Kingston's shoulder.

Oddly, she felt fondly for the two, and it seemed as though it were just yesterday when Kingston pleaded with her to enroll at the school.

Even with the setting sun, Kingston's brown eyes shone brightly as he nodded sharply at Mrs. Hats' words.

"I definitely will."

A smile crept onto her face. "Good, and one more thing. You need more practice at trying to hide your magical energy. The other teachers may have been fooled, but from the moment I set my eyes on you, I could tell you were outstanding. You did try though," she patted his shoulder.

With a playful wink thrown at Kingston,

Mrs. Hats loosened her grip on him before turning on her heel to leave and instructing the guards to give Kingston some time with his friends.

Kingston couldn't help but laugh. He thought he had fooled everyone at the school the entire time, but Mrs. Hats always knew he wasn't just an ordinary kid. She probably just waved it off seeing as she didn't sense anything evil from him.

"Make sure to eat good tasty meals all the time," Lisa instructed Kingston as she pulled at his cheeks.

Kingston nodded, unable to reply with how hard her pull on his cheeks was.

"And uh, don't talk to strangers too, you

might get hurt," Teddy added, his fingers fiddling with an item in his hands.

"I will," Kingston managed to say right before Lisa let go of his cheeks, allowing him to sigh out in relief.

"Same goes for you, Crowly," Lisa stated.

"You've got it, Lisa." Crowly replied.

"Good," Lisa grinned before rubbing Crowly's head.

There was an awkward silence as the group of friends all stared at each other before Lisa nudged Teddy, who quickly muttered an apology and handed Kingston a wrapped-up item.

"What's this?" Kingston asked, taking the item off Teddy's hands. It felt a bit heavy.

"A little something for you and Crowly to remember us by. I hope you like customized robes; it's kind of my style," Teddy said with a slight blush, waving to his robe which had unique markings on them, unlike those of other students.

"Thanks, guys," Kingston mumbled right before they parted from the hug.

"We've always got your back."

And so after the hug, Lisa and Teddy watched as Kingston walked away until they could no longer see him, and they headed back into the halls. Lisa sticking out her tongue at the guard who thought they'd end up in big trouble. She laughed when she saw the guard muttering something beneath his breath, and if it weren't for Teddy who nudged her forward to keep walking, she might've ended up teasing the guard more.

Everything ended rather well.

The kids were now recognized in school as heroes. And Mr. Dawson could no longer hurt innocent animals.

"We should come back here sometime and see them. I bet Lisa would've grown a tad bit taller then. Teddy's already tall enough as it is," Kingston commented, hopping over a large stone and heading back to the old forest where their real quest had first begun.

"I'm afraid Lisa might later turn into a bully. She scares me," Crowly confessed, wrapping his wings around himself as Kingston now walked through the long blades of grass, almost covering up his entire body.

The setting sun made everything around them look rather magical, and as usual, Kingston could imagine the sun grinning down at him.

"She already is a bully. My cheeks still hurt from how hard she pulled them."

But that was what made each of his friends unique. Lisa was the energetic one, always full of life and optimism. And there was Teddy. Quiet, a bit shy, but also brave. If it weren't for him speaking up at Mrs. Hats' office, things might have gone sideways. The kid also had a great fashion sense. Kingston was simply excited about what the robe Teddy had gifted him would look like.

As Kingston and Crowly continued their journey back to the forest, they thought about their quest to save the dragon.

Kingston laughed out loud at the memories of him trying to act as any ordinary student. There were many instances where he almost got caught. He also hoped that Bluey was doing fine and had been able to make some new friends in his new home.

Kingston would have preferred taking another route than that of the ancient forest, but he had totally forgotten to ask Mrs. Hats for a map.

The stars were now lining the skies by the time Kingston had returned to the dragon cove where they had first found the trail leading them out of the forest. Everything was as they remembered, and while Crowly went out in search of fruits for them to eat, Kingston opened up the item his friends had given him.

A letter first fell out before Kingston saw the red customized robe which Teddy had gifted him. There were also two books on advanced knowledge and a little brown scarf which had Crowly's name knitted on it in black. The handiwork was a bit messy, but Kingston was sure Crowly would burst out in tears at the sight of it.

After gently placing the items into his backpack, Kingston proceeded to open the letter to reveal two sets of messy handwriting clashing together at every point.

It read:

Dear Kingston,

Don't forget to eat some new food during your quests. You're a bit skinny, and if you had stayed with us a little longer, we'd have fattened you up. Thanks for joining us on your quest. We got to see a rare magical beast, so now we have something to boast about.

Kingston giggled. It sounded exactly

like something Lisa would say. Another horrible handwriting followed with a few words that ended the letter.

We will definitely miss you and Crowly. Though I still find it weird that he talks.

Right as he was finished with the letter, Kingston kept it safe in his backpack. He would make sure to add it to his box of memories back home. For now, he would make sure to read it every now and again and cherish the moments of his latest quest.

Crowly returned minutes later to find Kingston sprawled on the ground gazing at the night sky. He set the fruits he had picked up underneath his claws aside before settling down beside Kingston's head.

Kingston seemed happy, and seeing Kingston happy made Crowly feel content. They were best friends after all.

"So, what next, Kingston?" Crowly asked with a soft smile, and Kingston turned to face Crowly with a bright smile on his face.

"What do you think?" His grin grew wider. "We'll set off on our next adventure so we have lots of stories for Teddy and Lisa when we return."

The end.

Made in the USA
Las Vegas, NV
16 October 2024

96940416R00148